Beëlzebub's Bible

An Unholy Allegory

I0556254

Stephen Zoltan

Copyright

SPARSILE
BOOKS

Note:

This book is a work of fiction, building on previous works of fiction and fabrication. The views expressed herein do not necessarily accord with the views of the author or publisher. This work should not be taken as criticism of any real person, living, dead or undead.

The Bible of Babel

No-one thought the LORD GOD would just turn up one day and go on a downtown walkabout. After all, He hadn't been seen since biblical times. But when He finally turned up and set foot in the City to see for Himself, the people were filled with wonder and dread. People imagined the sky falling—towers crashing down—the city ruined—the end of civilisation. Never quick to reward human initiative, the Deity was ever suspicious of what man would get up to when left to his own devices. And this city is the greatest assembly of human devices ever devised. If anywhere demanded a personal visit from a curious, restless or disgruntled Almighty, then it was going to be here.

For this is the greatest city the world has ever known. It's the most artificial place—the most *human* place—on the face of the Earth. Drawing power, wealth and talent from all points of the compass, the city is like a vast overweening machine, improbably self-sustaining, feeding itself and consuming itself, churning frantically fast just to stay still; a restless society teetering from today into tomorrow.

At the top, the ruling classes and their entourages of advisers and hangers-on and celebrity astrologers and lifestyle gurus. And then the brash *nouveau riche* of the urban professional classes: the money-men and record-keepers and wheeler-dealers and pen-pushers. People living their artificial lives, knowing nothing of the toil of the land, their rustic past, of nomads or nephilim, or the humble earth from which they sprang. Then below all of them, there's the great mass of the sweating swarming metropolis, living for the buzz and bling and booty of the big city.

The city: where every kind of human desire is stimulated, indulged, flaunted, exploited, exhausted.

The city, where people invent sins faster than they can be forbidden.

In this age of atheism, the LORD God had, frankly, become a bit of an anachronism. Until this morning, He was lost from living memory. The days when God walked and talked with people seemed a million miles away, as if unreal: the stuff of myth. But today, since first light, there were rumours of the LORD stalking through the southern suburbs.

And the people were afraid.

But I was thrilled.

This could be the biggest story of my generation. The most shocking, awesome breaking news for centuries. And it's my job to write things down.

Yes, I am the first to be able to record it just as it happens. Balancing against the possibility that the world may be about to end, I am the first person to record an eye-witness account of the Deity in an urban environment.

~~~

As the Lord God advances upriver, He first passes orchards and fields of crops, then straggling rows of mean houses, with gritty gardens of stunted shrubs and a few blades of green, as if in mockery of a lost Eden. Then come the denser packed streets of the shabbier classes: grimy tenements, cold-water walk-ups, crowded bedsits and slums, rickety middens, hanging rags and scavenging animals.

Then He follows fetid-smelling river channels to the shipyards and quaysides, where He straddles ships laden with goods, and passes by the docks and the fish-market. In the streets, market traders, street performers, soothsayers, potion-merchants and moneylenders ply their trades. These days, property, debt and people are bought and sold just like goods or commodities. Meanwhile languid youths are hanging out in the squares, in small gangs, watching the girls go by.

As He pauses to take in the panorama of the premier city of the plain, there is so much for the Deity to catch up on. Bricks and mortar, for a start. Houses. Temples. Towers, walls and canals. In effect, just about everything

He can see, all those works of stone and wood, bronze and iron.

And peering closer down into the streets, all manner of inventions, of wheels and waggons, calculators and astrolabes, and in the markets, miscellaneous accoutrements of urban society—lutes and jewels and leather goods—all run on an uncanny contrivance of law and money, mathematics and writing.

A giant shadow falls across the city wall.

The LORD GOD is back.

And He is the talk of the town.

~~~

We're on Seth's roof terrace, at one of the more exclusive parties that night. We gaze out across the dusky sunset over the rooftops of the city, as we take in what could be our last night on Earth. A young lady with long dark eyelashes slithers past us on her way back from some nibbles, daintily fingering the sweet pastry flakes into her mouth. Serious-looking architects and astronomers are deep in conversation by the balustrade; under shady vines, financiers are rubbing shoulders with bohemians. All sorts of high flyers are here, from commodities traders to fashionistas and publisher types. There is a definite edge to the conversation, a sort of existential adrenalin-surge cutting through the collective consciousness of the chattering classes.

'To be honest, I always believed in God's role in history,' says a civil servant type, impeccably dressed, with a posh accent, nibbling some bread and hummus. 'But I thought His job was already done, in the past.'

The capitalisation of the divine pronoun is almost audible.

'Me too,' says Jared, my engineer friend, a level-headed hedonist, who nods seriously, and pops an olive into his mouth.

'Aren't you an atheist?' says Zillah, the girl with long dark eyelashes, who now latches on to our conversation.

Indeed, for a long time, people bored with their forefathers' stories had suggested that God didn't really exist. Or else, He must be tired—too old to act, or too old to think—after all, He must be over a thousand years old. Some had suggested that He was already dead—and there are not many uses for a dead God.

So most of us had got used to putting our day-to-day faith in humanity. God had handled Creation; fine, but now Earth is ours; what's more, this city is surely the biggest, brashest declaration of self-reliance, of human secession from divine tyranny.

'No, not an atheist, as such,' says Jared, with an air of measured self-revelation. 'Just a rationalist. Or to be more precise, an empiricist: going by the evidence that I can see for myself.'

And there are plenty of empiricists today, when you can see for yourself the transcendental heft of the LORD God clambering over the world's largest wall.

As for me, I got to know about God through school, by copying the Bible out on clay. Frankly, it was one of the less bothersome subjects—it wasn't like maths or astronomy; or even Language. Just the one skinny little text, of nine mercifully short chapters, ending with the rainbow. Nothing like the long drag of Gilgamesh. Our religious instruction was pretty light touch. The teacher just covered the basics: the Two Commandments; the First Amendment; and the Covenant.

Seth was pretty much the same—except he missed the day we did Chapter Three. As far as Seth was concerned, history went straight from the first couple to the first family, bypassing the Fall. The world still seemed to make sense this way. Seth's ever the optimist amongst us, always seeing the best in human—and divine—nature.

'I suppose you'll be busy writing something about all this?' says Seth, with a wolfish grin.

'Well, whatever happens, I'm ready for it.'

What is not certain is which God has turned up today. The Great Creator, who made the world, and breathed life into every living thing? Or the Almighty Destroyer, who nearly ended it all again?

~~~

And the Lord God inspects the walls of the city, the greatest thickest walls in the world: so wide that a team of horses and chariots can turn around on them. He seems to be admiring the sturdiness of the buttresses, the craft of the finishing, the uncanny order of straight lines. And the great Engineer looks down to inspect the canals, curious as to how similar they are to rivers, yet subtly their own thing. He is trying to fathom the ingenious balance of levels and flows of pressures that keeps all the water from just running away into the sea.

Then the LORD God pauses at the gates of the city. He fingers the indentations in the stone archway. It is an inscription. He pauses and sniffs. He seems puzzled, unsure of what to make of the lettering.

And now God is arriving at the Hanging Gardens. Here, right in the middle of the sultry city, he beholds a wooded hillside with shady arbours and streams. He perceives that it is a completely artificial landscape, with false ground levels, and pumped water flowing first uphill, then coming down again as gushing fountains. God must surely be secretly impressed by the extravagant ingenuity of the place.

And then God lifts his eyes to the horizon, and sees the new tower now taking shape on the skyline. It is the great Ziggurat, a magnificent monument to our city, and symbol of our times. It is a calculated investment in science, as it will serve as an observatory for our astronomers and astrologers, offering them new angles on the heavens.

The secrets of the sky yield before us. We have the measure of the major heavenly bodies—one for each day of the week. We know when the seasons start and end. We know when to expect the moon to eclipse the sun. And we know all about the constellations and the zodiac—we invented them.

The Ziggurat is not all about celestial mechanics. It will also act as an outlook tower: so we can see any enemies approaching for miles across the plain. Some whisper that the authorities could also use it to spy on dissidents within the city walls. Last but not least, the Ziggurat shall serve as an elevated refuge against inundation. Since the Covenant, we don't expect God ever to flood the world again. But—just in case.

~~~

Then Zillah has an idea.

'So if you're going to *write* about God's visit to the city, won't that be like creating a new bit of history that could go into the Bible?'

It was a neat idea, the Bible.

At first, written records were simply tallies of goods and IOUs—accounts of quantities of grain—or lists of kings, or battles won, stuff like that.

But then someone had the idea of recording all the old stories in the new media—tablets, text devices, whatever. I guess we're at one of those once-in-a-generation times when suddenly every story is being written down—or even, rewritten—for the new media.

Writing now includes the stories of our history, our very origins. And someone had the idea of putting them all together, each story a different chapter, more or less. But not only the stories: some genealogies, a bit of history and geography, that sort of thing. Some of it is a bit clunky, and some already out of date. But the human stories are pretty much timeless.

'What—you mean—that I could compose a new chapter for the Bible?'

In the old days, scribes were just used to encode facts and stories composed by others. But recently, writing itself is becoming to be seen as something creative. It's starting to take over what the storytellers always did. Before, they'd looked down on us scribes, as mere clerks, code-hackers, clay-gougers. But now, there's nothing to stop us crafting original stories ourselves. We're now part of the creative arts; some whisper that we could be putting traditional story-tellers out of business.

'Yes, just think, it could be a once-in-a-lifetime opportunity.'

It seemed a revolutionary possibility—to write up today's news as instant history, a factually accurate biblical account set in tablet form just as it happened.

'I can see it now,' says Seth, with a dreamy smile. 'It could be the triumphal tenth chapter, and the fulfilment of urban civilisation.'

'And it would be about *our* city,' says Jared, slapping the table.

'Yeah, it will beat anything written on Nineveh, or any Antediluvian city.'

'The city leaders will be pleased. Maybe give the scribes a pay rise!'

And we make a toast: 'To the scribes!'

'The new storytellers!'

'But seriously,' says Zillah with a sparkle of possibility in her eyes, 'the account you write could be as famous as the Garden of Eden…but this time, it would be the ultimate urban scene, the chapter to end all chapters.'

'Yeah, and we engineers could be in it—'

'And civil servants…'

'We could really make a name for ourselves!'

It feels indeed as if history is fermenting this night, and I am being thrust suddenly towards the beckoning edge of world literature.

~~~

As the day wears on, and God has not told us off or smitten anyone or knocked anything down, hopes are raised that things are going to be all right. The divine walkabout seems to be heading for a success. People gradually emerge back onto the sun-baked streets, to run errands, or swap gossip, while curious to catch a glimpse of the divine shadow, or even part of the divine person. There is a carnival atmosphere in the air. All over the city, preparations are being made to honour the Deity.

The state astrologer is taking no part in these proceedings. He is in disgrace. His department is employed, after all, to look out for exactly things like portents of doom, or the Deity doing a reccy. The beleaguered tabulators of omens are working away into the night, recalibrating the stars, updating their records of portents and effects, apprehensive for their own futures.

But the state theologian is roused into action. It's his job to make sure all the right rituals are observed. In the event, there is not much to be done. No-one needs reminding of the First Commandment. Human nature is already going forth and doing its multiplicative business in bedrooms and bowers around the city. The Second Commandment is an ongoing project; the growing evidence of our dominion over the earth all around us.

Then there's the First Amendment, which permits the eating of flesh. It is on this front that the theologian swings into action. His department prepares a magnificent sacrifice on behalf of the city. Butchers, bakers and chefs spring into action of royal and divine service. All round the city, the good citizens are doing their own bit to honour God, by throwing impromptu street parties and orgies. And, of course, barbecues. After all, the one sure thing known to please God is the savoury smell of grilled meat.

~~~

The sky has dimmed, and the darkness embraces the partygoers, as the glittering stars come out. Candle flames dance in the eyes of the guests. No-one is leaving. Everyone seems on a high.

'So what do you guys think God would have liked best?' asks Zillah, the light just then catching her sparkling eyes.

'Oh I dunno, the women?' says Seth, with a smirk. 'Or the canapés?'

'But seriously,' says Jared. 'The Canals, I'd have thought. In some cases, you can hardly tell the join, where God's handiwork stops, and ours begins.'

'Or maybe the Hanging Gardens?'

'True, they're quite something. You should see the hydraulics—'

'Forget the physics, think of the human story,' says Zillah.

The Hanging Gardens were said to be created by a lovesick king for his homesick Persian concubine, who longed for the verdant hills of home.

'You could say it's a re-enactment of Creation. A custom-built landscape, made for love. God would surely understand.'

'Or the Tower?' Seth suggests. 'There's nothing like it.'

'Or maybe He liked the mathematics,' says Zillah. 'Or the writing?'

'I'm not so sure,' I say. 'I'm not sure He could actually *read*.'

Indeed God seemed unsure, uncomfortable, suspicious of the writing. It was as if He was thinking: I gave them perfectly good voices and ears—why should they wish this contrived kind of communication? What are they up to this time? He seemed almost like a disgruntled parent whose children have invented a way of secretly communicating with each other via text messages behind his back.

'But He must be impressed with us for inventing it?' says Seth.

'I wouldn't bet on it. When did He ever reward human initiative, or us doing anything for ourselves?'

There's a long silence, as we think back through the nine chapters of biblical history.

We look out over the dark crimson sky and the cityscape in the cool of the evening, embraced by the warm hubbub of human voices, accompanied by the little clatters of plates and glugging of wine.

So far, so good. God has been on his best behaviour. There have been no temper tantrums, no toppling of towers, smashing of machines or burning of books. There has been no loss of life or limb; no hint of thunder, not a drop of rain.

But there's something strange in the air; something not quite right.

One of the guests, I think it's the civil servant—Arphaxad or Arpachshad—comes up and invites us to an orgy. At least that's what I think he's doing. Seemingly the worse for wear, he is gesticulating and grabbing me and Zillah by the arms. But he is slurring his speech, talking gibberish, and getting angry. We can't make him out. He looks baffled and offended, and goes off in the huff. There's a crash of crockery somewhere. I hear shouts and scuffles in the streets below. And this sort of unrest continues through the night.

~~~

Out here on the plains, we still hear of cities.

I can still read, but rarely write.

As it turned out, just one hurried line of mine made it into the Bible, about that fateful day when God came downtown to see the City for Himself.

In the end, He didn't think much of our civilisation.

He had grudging admiration for the engineering, but saw new rivers and hanging gardens as rather derivative, unnecessary contrivances. In fact, He always seemed cool about anything He hadn't invented Himself.

He didn't particularly appreciate all that technology making life easier than the toil He thought He'd had in store for us.

He didn't really get money. He liked the kebabs. He'd get back to us about the sex.

But He was apparently most disturbed by the writing. He'd always had a thing about knowledge and had devised ingenious ways of controlling it, through illicit trees and such-like. And on top of everything else, writing seemed to be another threat to this ancient order.

Even the Bible, He was not altogether happy with. Although transparently self-centred, He wasn't particularly keen on people taking down everything He said and quoting it back in His face. Maybe He came across as too wilful and capricious. Maybe there were not enough rules or rituals yet written into it. But anyway, the disadvantages must have outweighed the advantages. This writing business was obviously a step too far.

So he had to teach the people a lesson they'd never forget. *Thus the Lord came down and scattered the people and their tongues over the face of the Earth*. So the tale of Babel was not the end of history; more like the end of the beginning.

But in splintering civilisation, God has fractured his own future. The Bible of Babel was the first and last to involve all people of the world—and just the one God.

Heathen Eden

She lies there like a lioness, with her lithe limbs and tawny flanks, and two dark nipples. She is reclining after her lunch, in the drowse of a balmy afternoon, among the soft grass and wildflowers. She has this peaceful place to herself—or so she supposes. But a pair of eyes is watching her. The bald curves of her body alerted him: he has not seen such a creature before.

His gaze is curious, searching. He is drawn to study her face, but it's hard to place: soft-featured, pert, bright-eyed, sprite-like. There is something feral but familiar about her. He tries to fathom her age. His eyes glide down her front, lingering over her curiously fleshy chest then settling on her belly button.

So: the rumours must be true.

His mind races ahead, jumping to conclusions. But he has to let her know, now he has found her.

There is a sonorous plop as a fruit falls off an overhanging branch and into a tranquil pool. A fish stirs silently in the deep below.

She looks up, distracted momentarily, and lets her gaze linger around her, as if she senses she is being watched.

Just then, he rustles the branches and then bursts out into the sunlit meadow.

She looks around, but her surprise is mild, no more than that which a falling fruit would rouse in her.

A male figure stands before her, tallish, darkish, looking a little grizzled and careworn, as if he's lived a bit; but with a wiry strength and a certain pent-up poise.

'Eh, hello,' he says, smiling as good-naturedly as he can, voice wavering slightly.

'Hullo,' she says, with a little degree of curiosity, as if she is not too surprised to find strangers around the place.

'Eh, do you have a light?' He rummages in his kit of small-talk.

She looks around to left and right, as if to say where would she get a light from? 'Sorry.' And then continues, narrowing her eyes: 'Do I know you?' It's possible she could have seen him around these parts before.

'I, eh, don't know. I suppose not.' Their eyes make darting glances from one to the other. 'But I'd like to talk to you…'

She looks up as if to say, oh yeah?

'…To tell you about things, the world, you know.'

'I know about the world, and *things* already. I wasn't born *yesterday*,' she scoffs, looking down her very nakedly adult body as if to confirm it.

'Things you may not know about.'

'Don't you think I already know about the world? That night follows day, creeping things creep, and the earth is made of earth?'

'Look, I'm not doubting your knowledge of the world at large. But I've some more specific information, of a personal nature, to tell you.'

'Of a *personal* nature?'—she sits upright, now more awake than before. 'And sorry, but may I ask who you are? And what are you doing here?'

He's now looking at her just as keenly. 'I might ask the same of you.'

'Hey mister…I live here.'

There is definitely something rare and untamed about her.

'Okay, let me put it another way. Do you know who your parents are?'

That hits a chord. She is now looking him up and down keenly, her eyes fixing half-closed on him, as if he is on to something, and she needs to find what it is before he does. Then looks away.

'I don't *have* parents,' she says, airily, as if it would be the most natural thing not to have parents—like Aphrodite born out of the foaming churning sea.

He brings out some dried herbs and starts rolling up.

'All right, so do you know where you came from, then?'

No answer.

'Or why you are here?'

'What kind of question is that?' She now throws back her head, her silken locks brushing the tops of her shoulders. 'What about *you*?'

'We're all God's children,' he says carefully, if a little sheepishly.

'Well why did you ask, what everyone knows? You're going to tell me that God made everything, all this world for us to live in, obviously…' She gazes round the meadow, the tangled banks of fragrant flowers humming with insects, the trees hung with pears and pomegranates, and the pool stocked with fish.

He follows her gaze round the meadow and nods quietly.

'God made this world, that's true; but He didn't really create it for you.'

'Well, who did he create it for, then? Himself?'

'Ah now, it's not quite as simple as that. This world was first of all created for the animals: the beasts of the field, the birds and the bees…'

'Yeah, right, the world was made for the animals!'

'Look, obviously, God and the angels have Heaven to live in. But *Earth* was for the animals…and the plants, obviously—for the animals to eat.'

'So where do *I* fit in, then?'

He laughs, or more like winces. 'Good question.'

'Well?'

'Well…you don't, really. Fit in. You weren't exactly *planned* for. You were, well, more of an accident.'

'An accident?'

'You were, uh, conceived, unintentionally.'

Her eyes narrow momentarily, incomprehension curdling into suspicion for the first time. 'I was led to believe we were all…specially created by God.'

'Well, you are special, that's for sure—maybe even one of a kind. But you are not a pure creation, but a sort of hybrid.' He pauses to let her take this in.

'A hybrid?'

'You are half animal, half angel.'

A thought is dawning on her face. 'What? So my parents…?'

'Your mother was a beautiful creature, the fairest of animals…'

'And my father…are you saying was an angel?'

'A fallen angel, I fear.' And he takes a deep bow.

'And so…?' Her speech slips away as she gazes into space.

'I am your father.'

~~~

They face each other in silence, looking into each others' deep amber eyes.

'You…my father?'

'I'm afraid so.'

He is playing with some hemp leaves, distractedly. Then finally rolls up his joint, with obvious dexterity. She looks away, looks back, watches him. She is almost tempted to imagine him as her long-lost Dad, the dad she never had.

It's all very curious, but it's all so sudden.

'How do I know what you're saying is true? I mean, how am I supposed to know what an angel is, never mind what a fallen one looks like, in the flesh?'

'You just need to trust me…there are some things only I could know.'

'So…you must have known my mother?'

'I *knew* her, yes but…'

'What was she like, then?'

'You have to understand, I didn't know her for, uh, very long.'

'So, what *did* you know of her?'

'She was beautiful, of course,' he says, looking coyly at her sideways. 'Though not as—uh—beautiful as you.

She had a rougher hide, and a longer tail. She had, uh, personality...She could run pretty fast, too.'

'So, what became of her?'

'No-one knows. We can't know if she survived child-birth.' He looks down at the ground and shuffles uneas-ily. 'But no-one knew if any offspring could have lived. Until now.'

'So...I was *born*?'

'Exactly—what do you think that is?' Pointing to her belly button.

She looks down her front with a new curiosity; and he takes in her singular feminine form once more: with a sense of wonder and guilty pride in this exquisite living creature which somehow is the fruit of his own ugly deed.

'So hang on, how come no-one else told me this?'

'I guess they were embarrassed.'

'Embarrassed?'

'Embarrassed for me, embarrassed for you. I don't know, embarrassed for God. Of this whole new situa-tion—the human condition—that He hadn't planned. But still, I thought you ought to know.'

He breaks off to light up, and takes a long drag at his joint.

'I'd heard talk of "fallen angels", right enough,' she says, as her mind races. 'That might just make sense of a thing or two...'

'You'll have inherited my intellect, and a bit of guile, rebelliousness, maybe? So blame me, if you like, for any flaws.'

He shrugs and takes another puff. He can sense the worst is over.

'So…how did you find me?' she says.

He looks into the distance. 'Well, there were rumours…of this special kid, some curious hairless wonder that could walk, talk, and out-think every other earthly creature. Some thought it a myth, others didn't want to believe it. But it's easier to find something if you believe it exists. And more than anyone else, I had reason to believe you might really exist.'

'That figures, at least.'

'Feathers were ruffled in heaven, you can imagine. Your very existence upsets the balance of nature—a whole new kind of living being, in between the animals and the angels. They say that God was at first reluctant to let such a creature live, but became besotted by the myth of the double-breasted half-caste. But by acknowledging the little bastard, He'd be condoning, well, sexual transgression. The other angels were jealous, afraid that he'd love you that little bit more than them, despite your animal frailty. Or perhaps even because of it.'

'Animal frailty?' She stares at him. 'What kind of animal frailty?'

He shrugs. She doesn't look convinced by his reticence.

'I…I suppose it's possible you are mortal.'

'What does that mean?'

'It means you could die, at any time, forever.'

'You mean, like, cut down like a flower? No more blessed than any wretched beast in the field?'

'I'm afraid so. But hey—who knows if you're mortal, until you die? It's all new territory. For all I know, you could have the best of both worlds. My brains and your mother's looks.'

She stifles a wry smile. He takes a puff.

'And what if the worst of both worlds?'

'Well…You could end up with all the physical frailty and cravings of animals; but the moral hang-ups of the angels. You could end up mortal like an animal, but with the angels' knowledge of mortality…'

The tragedy of the human condition. The only wretched creature to be mortal and to know it.

There's another splash as another fruit plunges into the pool.

'Don't get me wrong, the angels are well-meaning, their morals are all well and good—for celestials living in heaven. It's easy for them to turn their noses up at the pleasures of the flesh. But it's your animal birthright to enjoy those things.'

'Hmm. So is there such a thing as an angel birth-right?'

'Eh, I'm not sure you can bank on that. Being the feral lovechild of a fallen angel probably doesn't get you many rights. You're probably better off where you are. At least here you can still lord it over the animals, rather than being the lowest of the low, if you were among the angels.'

'Lower even than a fallen angel?'

'I'm afraid so.'

'And what then should I do?'

'Now that's a question.' He pauses, and takes another drag of his joint. 'Maybe it's a bit late to be giving you father's advice…' He sighs.

'No, please. Go right ahead.'

'Well, since you may be mortal…If I were you, I'd live from day to day as if I could die any time. Eat, drink and be merry. Find yourself a lover. Be fruitful and multiply. You've got the God-given body for it…'

He offers her some weed. This time, she takes it. After all, it's only another innocent little plant from God's garden.

He lights up, and they each take a drag, then exhale together.

~~~

He looks out into the distance, beyond the meadow to the heath and scrubland beyond. It's beautifully harmonious and blissfully wild at the same time.

'I suppose I ought to go now.' He gives her a tentative hug. 'But at least I've done what I had to do. You're an adult now. You can take your own decisions...'

As she takes in his unaccustomed advice, she wonders if those words mean he's finally claiming fatherly responsibility, or finally releasing himself from it.

'...so you can do exactly as you desire.'

His eyes look long into hers, and he gently cups her face with his hand, as if looking for a reaction.

She holds his gaze defiantly, and breathes out some smoke.

'I've been with men before, you know. Well, a man, at least.'

'Oh, really?' he says, as casually as he can. 'Eh, what's a man?'

'The male of the species. Just some other hybrid like me, no doubt.'

Uh-oh—so there's another one...

'When you say he's like you, do you mean physically, mentally, or...?'

'Our bodies fit each other, if that's what you mean. But not our personalities. He thought he was superior to me. Always wanted to be on top, you know?' She raises an eyebrow. 'So I left him. I'm not anyone's underling. Not then, not ever. Just so you know.'

She looks him in the eye; and takes a last drag, and looks away again.

'So I *am* free to do exactly as I desire.'

'And what of that…man?'

'Oh, he's been domesticated now. God arranged for him a new little wife. Yeah, they live in a garden.'

She stubs out her joint. 'I mean, I could accept being told I was God's long-lost lovechild. But I don't fancy being His live-in livestock. I'd rather take my chances out here.'

She turns to him then. 'But hey, why don't you check them out? Go to their little garden and try your stories on them?'

The Serpent's Footprints

Of all the revelations of the Age of Science, none has been so celebrated nor far-reaching as the recent discovery of the location of the Garden of Eden. The portentous unearthing of this location of legendary deception has not only revised the geography of Creation and the history of Man, but has literally rewritten the pages of Scripture. The breakthrough was occasioned by the unprecedented discovery of paleontological evidence of the biblical Serpent.

From early times, merchants trading in the hinterland of what we now identify as Eden had stimulated interest in exotic fruits and artefacts found in that region. Ground-down bones of creatures thought to be extinct since the Flood added a frisson of the exotic, with their supposed aphrodisiac qualities of obscure, even unnatural provenance. This stirred the curiosity of a Scottish explorer and sometime scholar named McBridie, a singular individual with an insouciant intellect, locally celebrated for having once attempted to trace the source of the West Nile using only a street map.

On an otherwise idle afternoon in the library that now bears his name, McBridie was struck by the thought that no-one seemed to have ever ascertained the true geographical location of the biblical Eden. Over supper, he dreamed up his ingenious plan, to trace the courses of the four great rivers of Paradise: the Tigris, Euphrates, the Pishon and Gishon. Like a latter-day Lunardi, McBridie would make an ascent by hot-air balloon, and pass over the mountains of the Levant and the plains of Mesopotamia. From his lofty vantage point, McBridie would be able to view with effortless advantage certain topographical features in the landscape that had hitherto been unremarked from the ground, and would lead him inexorably to the location of the first home of Man.

After just a few days in a now arid zone around the headwaters of the Pishon, McBridie was to discover in some rocky escarpment the imprints of mysterious reptilian feet, which could only be supposed to be those of the biblical Serpent. McBridie's felicitous breakthrough was, of course, founded upon the logical inference that if the Serpent was at the Fall condemned to go upon its belly, it must previously have had limbs, and by extension, feet. McBridie instinctively realised that this discovery would provide the missing link between terrestrial science and biblical reality.

Whereas McBridie's only previous publication, *Travels in the Vicinity of Havilah, Cush, Assyria and Mesopotamia* had been a somewhat solipsistic dissertation meeting with limited appeal, his new work, written up as *The Vestiges of Eden*, swiftly ignited the public imagination of the day. McBridie's magisterial study was to become celebrated in the drawing rooms of London, Paris and St Petersburg. His bound volume of printed maps and lithographs—famously depicting not only the topography of Eden but the magical reality of its flora and fauna—stimulated a new fashion for intellectual pilgrims to find scientific enlightenment of the works of Creation in the land where Man first trod the Earth.

Spurred on by McBridie's success, all manner of scientific investigations rapidly followed. A team of Assyrian archaeologists, rediscovering the inference that Eden was bounded, were able to posit evidence for the first ever Walls, of the first Garden. Evidence of the first man-made constructions at first proved more elusive, although a bold architectural historian was able to infer the existence of Adam's house—and sundry items of furniture—in paradise. A Prussian anthropologist painstakingly articulated evidence of the first ever garments, made (it will be recalled) by God from skin—rumoured to be left over from an earlier, unsuccessful act of Creation. A team of Ottoman hydrologists were able to fearlessly extrapolate, in their laboratory, the atmospheric conditions for the mist that watered the earth before the first rain. A husband and wife team of meso-American palaeontologists dexterously crystallised evidence for the fossilised teeth of vegetarian lions. Their current audacious line of enquiry is to seek direct paleontological evidence of the footprints of God.

McBridie's success also inspired the advancement of antediluvean zoology; in the seeking out of evidence for certain corrupt creatures—hybrids and monstrosities—that were regarded as potential threats to the stable order between Man and Beast, and that had to be destroyed in the Deluge. The antediluvian zoologists seek the fossil traces of such creatures as sphinxes and the offspring of Nephilim and human females. Most controversially, some sages believe that God—whose doctrine at the time, it will be recalled, favoured fruitful intercourse among all living things—first tempted Adam to have sexual relations with the animals before creating a female companion for him.

Arboriculturalists have sought to identify the botanical properties of the Tree of Life and the Tree of the Knowledge of Good and Evil. The more conservative scholars believe that there has only ever been one such tree of each kind. An increasing number of radical thinkers believe that these trees have naturally borne seed and yielded myriad descendants down the generations, and live among us yet today. We eat unheedingly of their fruits: one fruit temporarily bestowing immortality; the other, just as surely, condemning us once more to mortality. Thus is explained the bittersweet existence of the human condition.

Meanwhile, silviculturalists speculate on the existence of other enchanted trees: many otherwise unexplained phenomena could be more credibly understood by the posited existence of a Tree of Reason, a Tree of

Language and a Tree of the Knowledge of Self. All the available evidence suggests that men and women were intended to eat—and have since duly consumed—the fruits of these trees. As far as we know only one species, among the animals, is definitely known to have partaken of all three of these potent plants.

Indeed, the most fascinating of creatures of Eden is the Serpent, which zoologists now recognise as possessing the faculties for reasoning and self-knowledge—the latter being inferred, not least, from its capacity for deceit. A third property is not the result of the Serpent eating enchanted fruits, but by its encouragement of others to do so. This precipitated the great change in its circumstances of life, from having first been like any other reptile equipped with four limbs, to afterwards being condemned to slither along the ground on its belly. Modern men of science, incidentally, believe the loss of limbs was not necessarily immediate; but was no less real for that. Palaeoserpentologists continue the search for further evidence of the fossilised footprints of the original quadrupedal proto-serpents.

~~~

With every discovery of modern science, the natural unity of knowledge of the world is ever more greatly reinforced. Each new breakthrough helps confirm, illuminate and elaborate what was known before. By the marvel of modern scholarship, the fusion of Science and Natural Theology can reveal that all phenomena and events are related. It is by no accident that science and scripture should converge on the same great story of Life and the history of the World.

Only the irrational remain in sincere denial; contrarians and heretics are derided for their refusal to believe the evidence of science, which clearly proclaims the magnificence of Creation. Only the satirists receive any attention for articulating subversive alternatives to accepted doctrine. Imagine, they say, if the relative motion of the spheres and passage of the stars in their courses could somehow cast doubt upon the immovability of the Earth, rather than confirm it. Imagine if the discovery of strange new species of creeping thing should not proclaim the Creator's greatness, but should somehow diminish it. Or imagine if the discovery of some old bones in some old stones, instead of attesting to the glorious foresight of their Creator, should somehow bear witness against Him.

Indeed, it is only in children's stories that ideas more absurd than these may be found: the recently rediscovered *Fingal's Fables*, depicting the tale of a lost society of hairy animals that lived before the first men; and McBridie's own gothic tale of *Gastronomia Horribila*, where vile flesh-eating predators stalk the early Earth, adulterating their diets with animal flesh, instead of eating fruits and leaves.

Both devout and free-thinking scientists believe the Creator has written in the great Book of Nature solemn and compelling testament to the meaning, history and (some believe) destiny of this world. Conversely, the great truths of Nature are explained—in such a concise form—in the pages of scripture. Over time, therefore, it became natural that the Age of Science and God-given Reason should give stimulus to a radical new idea: the Scientific updating of Scripture.

It was truly an idea whose time had come; though, strange as it may seem now, at the time the conservative theologians at first believed that Scripture should remain untouched. But the progressives argued that the living text of the Word should be updated according to the times. It is not as if the new scientific evidence could conceivably contradict the essential truth of the Bible, they argued; but rather that some details not present in the original could augment and elaborate it, with the new revelations that Science now casts upon the story of the World.

After all, the Bible, though divinely inspired, reaches us—as any true scientist and devout lover of knowledge must understand—through the imperfect medium of human agency and the fallible hand of man. Scripture is not immaculately conceived, so this argument goes, but embodies the best translation of the soundest recollection of what the ancient prophets and their followers would have said and written. After all, the memories of three-hundred-year-old men are not wholly dependable. It is possible that Adam and his fellow narrators might have been confused about the exact order of the events of Creation. The dialogue of those first days in

Eden might be imperfectly remembered: even while the essential message of conversations with the person of God, which Adam directly experienced in his youth, must have remained vivid, the exact words might be inaccurately recalled in old age.

In the circumstances, it is eminently reasonable that scientific theologians should seek to update Scripture in line with the revelations of Science, and thereby uphold the natural unity of the understanding of the Universe. After all, the very first bible would naturally have been factually up to date. Why would we not use the hard-earned knowledge of our own day to fortify the living text of the greatest Book of all ages? To do otherwise would be a gross heresy, implying that the Bible was merely a literary relic, a work true to its time but belonging in the past—or, worse, a treatise positively incompatible with contemporary knowledge.

Thus did the scholars of the new scientific scripture go to work.

~~~

Genesis was the first book up for revision. The apparent incongruity of the sun's creation—after two days and nights have already passed—is deftly resolved by the insertion of a new verse on celestial mechanics. Some small but substantive textual amendments ensure that the order of appearance of plants, animals and humans is clarified. And the subtle but fundamental discrepancy between the domesticated environment of the Garden and its wilder environs is more firmly adduced.

The egregious passage featuring the originally simultaneous advent of the first man and first woman—that had fuelled rumours of Adam having a first wife, before Eve—was duly expunged, while the unhelpful conjecture of feral humans not descended from Adam is judiciously suppressed in footnotes. The shadowy agency of angels—practising and fallen—is now more explicitly cited to help explain the behaviour of mortals. And vivid new passages are provided to explain original vegetarianism, the inadvertent invention of sexual intercourse, and the fine line, in those heady early days, between incest and bestiality.

The nature of the mist (that occurred before the first rain) and the acoustic properties of divine footsteps now appear in marginal notes. Maps depicting the geography of Eden are inserted, to augment the traditional cartography of the Holy Land. The most sumptuous editions contain facsimiles of McBridie's original lithographs. Meanwhile, new passages on botany and silviculture are added. The arboreal habitat of Genesis now features Trees of Reason, Language and Self-Knowledge: the edibility of the fruits of these trees helps to explain not only man's condition, but the behavioural capacities of the Serpent. Last but not least, the bible's astronomical knowledge is brought a bit more up to date by adding in the cosmology of ancient Babylon as an Appendix.

In the retrospect of his after-supper reverie, McBridie reflected on the revealed nature of scientific discovery. It will be recalled that it would be McBridie's ground-breaking exposure of that single set of reptilian footprints that ignited the great efflorescence of scientific inquiry into territories scriptural, which continues to this day. But with hindsight, it did not require McBridie to make the effort of traversing the Holy Land, to unearth his serendipitous evidence, for the fateful seduction of Scripture by Science to be so boldly and irrevocably consummated. With hindsight, all that it would have taken was for men of science—and no less, men of religion—to have had the sufficient audacity of faith, that Genesis was indeed historical fact, to pursue the necessary evidence and textual revision to their logical conclusion. But then, a world bent on self-deception has no need of a serpent, nor trace of its footprints.

The Cosmic Hinterland of History

Moral Hazard

A sharp rap at the door makes him start. In these dark days, any visitor could spell trouble for John Milton. At worst, he has been betrayed by his publisher, and this could be dark forces arriving to haul him off to face a traitor's death. At best, it is Mr Simmons visiting to announce that he'd publish his new history, his latest and greatest work. In an eternity of seconds, Milton's mind races: is it to be the churning of printing presses or the rattle of disembowelling cutlasses?

The reality is more humdrum—the publisher politely returning the manuscript to the author.

'To be honest, I don't know what to make of it.' The publisher speaks bluntly. 'Is it a history or is it a fantasy? Or a satire, masquerading as truth, perhaps?'

'It is a history,' Milton returns, pointedly, 'as I believe is clearly indicated on the title page.'

'If it is history, it is incredible. If it is a fantasy, it is blasphemous. And as satire, it is seditious. What were you thinking of? Are you out of your mind?'

There is an uneasy silence.

Then Simmons continues more gently. 'This manuscript may spring from a brilliant imagination, with the craft of a poet, and the zeal of a pamphleteer. But it is not history. I can't publish this, as you must surely know. If anything, I'm doing you a favour by not burning it immediately, before getting us both arrested and carted off to the Tower!'

These are troubled times, when rumours swirl of clandestine agents of church and state bent on silencing heliocentric heresies, and rogue Royalists exacting retribution on those on the losing side in the civil war. In this most righteous corner of Christendom, a one can be executed for denying the Trinity.

Still, Milton trusts his old collaborator implicitly. It isn't that Samuel Simmons is so pious as to be timid in a publishing sense; but there is no market for the wrong kind of heresy.

'I'm sorry if my humble history has disturbed you, Mr Simmons. Yet I swear, sir, that it is as historically accurate as is humanly possible to record.'

'But, Mr Milton, I always thought you as devout as any man. Not exactly orthodox in your beliefs; but at least, holding beliefs that range within the compass of Christendom. Are you sure of what the manuscript says?'

The publisher is well aware that since going blind, Milton needs the services of an amanuensis to write down his words; and his uncomfortable insinuation is that this circumstance could bring room for error, or even deceit.

'I have every confidence in the reliability of my scribe, sir. The text has been read back to me, several times, and I have no doubt about its content.'

The publisher sighs and then reads out the opening passage:

'The world is not, as we have long supposed, God's primary creation. After Chaos, Heaven and Hell, Earth is but the fourth realm. What is more, Man was not the first sentient being, created a matter of days from the beginning of Time; but entered the world long after Celestial Beings had already established societies, language, politics, industry and mechanics; before a single naked human trod the Earth. The Fall of Man—'

Then Milton cuts in, repeating from memory, perhaps with a little pride:

'...was not a chance encounter between an ingenuous human and a dissembling reptile; but was a calculated act of sabotage, just the latest engagement in a much larger war in which battle-hardened angels ranged their celestial weaponry against the devilish engines of the infernal legions.'

'But John, this is preposterous! It is all very well to claim the Earth goes round the Sun, well, that is controversial, yes, very fashionable. But *this*…If the good Lord Himself had proclaimed that Hell was above and Heaven below, I should scarcely have been more shaken.'

'Nevertheless,' continues Milton, 'however *unorthodox* it may be, do you not find my narrative coherent, and consonant with reality? You will admit that not one word of it contradicts scripture. Nor, for that matter, the revelations of science. My history merely elaborates our existing knowledge, illuminating it from new perspectives. But do you not see that it also *integrates* history, science and scripture, in an original way—something that I had hoped a perceptive publisher might appreciate.'

'I grant you that it has a consistent *tissue* of circumstances, and some intriguing details that almost sound first-hand. Why, it is as if some bold traveller had himself ascended to the heavens, like a latter-day Icarus, and undertaken a survey of…the Circumfluous Waters… or a traverse of Transpicious Space? But if you did not see for yourself the shores of the Sea of Jasper beyond the celestial spheres, or fabricate the Causeway across Chaos in your own imagination, how did you come by such information?'

The Celestial Delegation

I perceived three exceedingly tall persons, unusually widely set, stooping or rather contorting themselves to get through the door. I noticed the quietly firm tread of bare feet, and there was a gentle flapping of air as they brushed past me.

I had been naturally disturbed to have unannounced strangers knocking me up, out of my after supper slumber; but was disarmed by the serenity of their greeting and graciousness of bearing. The leading figure had greeted me in Latin; but in a strange accent. Not English—but not Roman, either.

'I am the archangel Raphaël,' said the first. 'And these are Ithuriel and Zephon, my assistants, pastoral and pedagogical. We have come to tell you of the Heavens and the Earth.'

Angels! Appearing to me. Here in London. Now, in the seventeenth century!

'Uh…well, welcome…What do you want of me?'

I confess that my first impulse was to wonder if I might be receiving tidings of the Second Coming.

'We suppose that you are intending to write a history, and we have some technical information that might be of use to you.'

'Technical information?'

'Yes,' he continued, affably. 'Technical information about celestial motions'—I sensed a waving of arms. Or wings—'You will be aware, of course, of the lights in the sky; the greater and lesser lights, and so on and so forth…'

'Yes, of course. As it is written in Genesis…'

Then Zephon cut in, with a querulous burr, saying, 'And you may also be aware of the egregious conjectures of Bruno, and Galileo?'

Bruno had been burnt at the stake for his heresy; Galileo spent his last years as a prisoner of the Inquisition.

'Well, I have visited Italy, but—'

'You do not deny that you have met Galileo?'

'No—yes. Well…' One had to watch one's words these days. I wondered what would happen if one lied to an angel. 'I thought that Galileo's theory might be useful to my history. But I am aware that it is only one theory.'

'Quite so. *Only a theory*. And it shall best remain so,' warned Zephon.

'Indeed, you need not be concerned if the Sun rise on the Earth, or the Earth rise on the Sun,' resumed Raphaël. 'Whether the geocentric or heliocentric hypothesis is true, the position of the Heavens furth of the starry spheres remains intact beyond that. There is no need to solicit further things which the great Architect had wisely concealed.

'You understand that scripture cannot mention every little celestial detail. We believed it was sufficient to sketch out the origin and basic disposition of the, ah, major elements. Our mortal audience prefers the narrative to go as directly as possible to those beings most like themselves.'

'An earlier draft, sir,' cut in Zephon, somewhat sniffily, 'indeed contained more detailed explanation of astronomical matters.'

'Things that were not mentioned in scripture?'

'Some things are simply too great for human minds to comprehend,' added Raphaël, matter-of-factly. 'And this is why we did not earlier divulge such matters cosmological and astronomical and so forth. But now, since the new discoveries of this age of Science, we felt that Man might be ready to receive more technical revelations about the heavenly bodies, which would attest yet more strongly to the grandeur of the great Creator's almighty works.'

'This is most intriguing,' I replied, 'but what manner of things did you have in mind?'

Zephon sighed impatiently, as if ever having to explain such points to lesser souls, venturing, 'So, take for example, after the Fall, we arranged for the axes of the Earth to be tilted, so that the eternal spring of Paradise was replaced by the seasons you have known since. This explains how you come to have freezing winter and scorching summer.'

Then the sumptuous voice of Ithuriel intervened. 'You must imagine that Adam and Eve would have been too busy just getting used to their own bodies—their feelings—their relations with other creatures—to be thinking of such abstract things as axes and zeniths and azimuths. Remember, they had never even been outside their Garden. They knew nothing of the bounds of their world—the trackless deserts, the fathomless seas—far less the axial rotation of an oblate spheroid in space.'

'But now Men—and you in particular, Mr Milton—are in a better position to understand the almighty works of the Heavens,' said Raphaël. 'And so we shall be most grateful to you, sir, if you should now write this up for us so that people on Earth will better understand these multifarious works of God.'

My heart was racing, my mind eager.

'Do you mean that you are commissioning me to write new passages of Scripture?'

'Ah, no; we simply wish that you write your History in such a way that men are well aware of the divine provenance and indeed prescience of these almighty works, expressly including those most recently discovered by modern ways.'

And Raphaël clasped my hand, earnestly. 'Think not that mere rationality of thought could cause revolution in the heavens. Your mission shall be to show that science is not revealing anything not already known to men of God.

'And be careful to shun any who would try to pervert or deny the veracity of Scripture.'

This lofty admonition would be tested sooner than I expected.

An Unexpected Debt

We took our places either side of the fireside, and exchanged small-talk about the affairs of the world, the civil war, the price of beer. I had got used to the tread of angels' feet in my home. But this time was diffcrent.

For a start, there was this faintly unpleasant smell, which at the time I could not quite place. Then, there was my new visitor's general tone. He didn't have that earnest serenity of the angels I had come to be familiar with. He seemed more pugnacious, restless, and strangely curious.

'But did they actually tell you anything new?' he asked in a gravelly baritone.

'Well, to be honest, a lot of it I already knew from the King's Bible. But they did tell me a few new things—like how the angels created the seasons.'

'So they let you into that little secret, then. But did they tell you any really controversial things, like the Earth going round the Sun?'

'Actually, now you come to mention it, they steered me away from that. They said that the heavens are above and beyond all that sort of thing. They said…something about Transpicious space and Circumfluous waters located beyond the furthest starry sphere.'

'Typical!' he spat, with patent scorn. 'They're so evasive. They only tell you the absolute minimum, and half the time in riddles. It's a classic tactic to keep the people in the dark.'

'So…have you come to enlighten me?'

'Yes, and it's about time that you heard it from my side of things.'

'What do you mean, your side of things?'

'Well, have you never heard of the rebel angel who rose up to defy the tyranny of heaven?'

And it hit me—the smell—sulphur—my jaw dropped involuntarily and a gut feeling lurched in my stomach like a trapdoor below the gallows.

'So. You have heard of me, at least,' said the voice. 'Be not afraid,' he added, with impeccable etiquette. 'This is a personal visit. Do you mind if I smoke?'

My mind raced, my imagination running ahead of my fear. The image of a white-breasted feathery-winged angel dissolved and reformed into a ghastly vision of a dark ruddy horned figure, his face all scorched and flushed, with blazing eyes, lighting up and puffing on his cigarillo, with sinister hook-fingered wings like a bat, flapping horribly in front of the fireplace. For God's sake, maybe a scaly skin, maybe a slithery tail!

I tried not to shrink physically from him. I smelt the puff of tobacco smoke and a whiff of sulphur waft across to me.

'But, why—wh-what do you want of me?'

Here I had the very Devil making himself at home in my own house! What if he wouldn't leave? Or—what if he wanted to drag me back to Hell? I became newly aware of the heat of the fire crackling and spitting in the hearth.

'I heard you were writing a book. I heard you were talking to angels. I get around. So I thought you could do with hearing my point of view. Do you wish to know about the true state of Creation?'

'Uh…yes. Yes, by all means, whatever you wish…'

My voice was steadying, but my heart was still racing.

He reached for my bottle of wine, and poured us each a measure; I was too scared to think or do anything but accept. And so it was that I found myself drinking with the Prince of Darkness.

'I think it only fair that history records events from my side of things for a change. But I thought maybe you could make some grand narrative out of it.'

By now, the wine must have steadied my nerves, or at any rate my journalistic instincts had stirred into action. My curiosity dissolved any fear of corruption by a diabolical blasphemy.

'Well, I can certainly try.' If God should spare me…

'Indeed, I should be indebted to you. I've had too much nonsense written about me. But you! I expect you to produce a proper account of Heaven and Hell, from a first-hand informant…' and he took a great drag from his cigarillo, and exhaled another sulphury gust '…unless, of course, you'd care to visit the World Below to see for yourself…?'

I assured him I would be happy to make use of anything he could tell me.

'I can do better than tell you,' he said. 'I have taken the liberty to prepare—or have my minions prepare—my own little historical account. It started out as a modest biography, but as I found my life story bound up with the destiny of the worlds, it became more of a history as it went along, and ultimately a whole cosmography. Still, I suppose that I am the central character. You may use as much of this material as you wish, in order to get my point of view across, albeit without revealing my input. I leave it in your hands.'

And with another sulphury gust, he was gone—and a skin-bound, papery manuscript fell into my lap.

The Lost Book of Satan

Satan's narrative must have shocked in proportion to the degree that it enlightened. Satan—or one of his literary minions—may not have been a writer of the first rank, but his tale did not lack drama, a wealth of intriguing details, nor a certain degree of passion. Here we are told a story with many things missing from official Scripture; a story that had never before been told to mortals. We can summarise the gist of the tale, which can in any case be inferred from *Paradise Lost* itself.

Satan's was a protracted narrative about the beginning of Creation, and the society of Heaven; his early life and later rebellion, and being cast into Hell; how he built up his own infernal empire, and assembled his council in Pandemonium. There is an explanation of Satan's relations with Heaven and the denizens of Hell; the miraculous begetting of a daughter, Sin, and their incestuous offspring, Death.

And he told of a violent, war-torn heaven, in which angels had no qualms about resorting to violence to prosecute pitched battles with Satan's rebellious legions; how Satan's troops had invented many machines of war, but the heavenly hordes responded with offensive weapons of their own. He told how his insurrection failed, but the heavenly victors had not quite finished their enemy off. In fact the angels were horrified that Satan was left in place, seemingly free to travel about in his own dominions, and interfere on Earth, even if debarred from entering Heaven. And he told of the long cold war that followed since, hostilities limited to acts of espionage, occasional skirmishes, and a persistent battle of propaganda between the opposing sides.

And Satan told of how he heard rumours of a new project, of God's plans to create a new World. So Satan decided to get back at God, by attacking his latest pet project, this new world, that is Earth. He told how he became incarnate, and visited the terrestrial World, including Paradise—corrupting it almost as soon as it had been inhabited. Sin and Death were unleashed on the world, and thence a bridge was constructed across Chaos to expedite communication between Hell and the

World; the Earth became a tributary possession of Hell, as much as a nominal province of Heaven.

The narrative provides little insight into the first humans. It seems that Satan thought little of them. At the time, of course, they were just some unidentified new species on an uncatalogued planet. Adam and Eve come across as meek actors, with little personality—like some defenceless herbivores, too naïve for their own good, and almost in need of someone to come along and wise them up about the realities of the world. They were always just pawns in a larger game. After all, the primary target of Satan's offensive was not Adam and Eve, but God.

And then we have the star of the show himself. What a magnificent character is Satan! Even in the third-hand account of *Paradise Lost*, the power of his character still blazes through. We can sense Satan revealed in his full errant glory: proud, defiant, wilful, obstinate, disobedient, greedy, clever, conniving, arrogant, ambitious; but also having initiative, resourcefulness, and a degree of personal bravery. He even has moral qualms—as when he weighs up the fate of what will befall his victims. So we can simultaneously be drawn to him and repulsed, because we see in him the best and worst of ourselves. The point here is not that Satan is justified or commendable. Rather it is that Satan is a closer analogue of ourselves than any other who lived before the Fall.

And this, of course, explains our enduring fascination with Satan. Milton's transcription gives us the most original and vivid depiction of Satan as the first fully rounded *human*. If we recognise ourselves more fully in Satan than in Adam and Eve before the Fall, it must be because Adam and Eve were then as blank canvases, waiting to be written on. Satan has, in a sense, made us in his own image.

The Fall was Satan's own act of Creation.

Publish or be Damned

'So you can see my dilemma,' Milton explains to his would-be publisher. 'I am in a precarious position. On the one hand, the angels expect me to write up my history, with certain heavenly updates added in. If I publish that, I may be accused of heresy by Church or State, for the impertinence of latter-day prophesy. If I cannot get it past the censor, or leave it unpublished, I will incur the displeasure of my celestial sponsors. On the other hand, the Devil himself has bent over backwards to supply me with his own story, and exhorted me to publish his side of events, events which are so shocking that they would exile me from society, never mind the favour of Heaven. But then again, if I don't publish, I shall have Hell to answer for.'

Simmons fidgets, sighs and pauses. 'I would like to help you out, of course, but...well, this is dangerous stuff! People have burnt for less than this!'

'Listen, Samuel, if this work should remain unpublished, it should not reflect well on my *publisher*, should it?'

'But look…it's blasphemous…heretical…diabolical…!'

'And yet, no less true for all that,' says Milton with steely calm.

'But John, is the Devil's testimony really reliable?'

'I suppose, if you think about it, Satan is the one witness with first-hand experience of all four realms: Heaven, Hell, Chaos and the Earth. Nothing he said contradicts any evidence we have of our world around us, nor what the angels said. In fact, in some ways it makes more sense of scripture. Dare I say, it gives a bigger picture than scripture.'

'I suppose so. But then, Satan's information about Hell is not positively corroborated by anyone else. He could have just invented the tale of his infernal empire, for all we know. What if Satan was a fantasist?'

The publisher drums on the manuscript with his fingers.

'And anyway…is it ethical to use material furnished by the Devil?'

'Well, as Satan said: if the Devil's testimony should shed new light on matters celestial, then it should surely serve to magnify the works of God, even if the angels had not thought fit to mention it? That should surely please Heaven…'

'I suppose so.'

'And it could be our big chance in this world, here and now. This work would sell across Christendom. It should appeal to all sorts of Christians—and even Catholics. We could surpass Dante.'

'Surpass Dante…'

Simmons' mind is racing, calculating; and his fingers drumming.

'So will you publish it?'

'I think I can see a way that we can…But it will need some changes.'

Afterword

And so it came to pass that Milton rewrote his opus, not as a History, but as an epic poem. *Paradise Lost* was published by Samuel Simmons in 1667. The poem, insofar as it agrees with Scripture, means the author could not be accused of heresy. Presented as a dramatic fiction, it would not risk Milton having to disclose his sources, or be suspected of intercourse with the Devil.

The poem is a tragedy which plumbs the cosmic hinterland of history, going higher and deeper and earlier than the Bible. Compared with Milton's lost History, the actually published poem is less concerned with the cosmography and the worlds, but focuses more on the personalities, and the unfolding story of humanity; though it contains plenty of vestiges of the original.

For Milton cleverly drew from some of his own conversation with the angels to craft the dialogue between Adam and Raphaël, putting his own questions and reactions in Adam's mouth. And he did not hesitate to fabricate additional scenes with Adam and Eve revelling in each other's company, to appeal to his human readership.

To satisfy the censor, Milton made clear that God Himself is above the fray, always mindful of what is going on. Indeed, He knowingly foresees the whole tragic tale—while absolving Himself of any blame in advance. Meanwhile, Satan is shown to have sown the seeds of his own destruction.

The portrayal of Satan himself remains compelling. Satan more or less steals the show, and is almost the real tragic hero of the piece. Milton of course benefited from first-hand knowledge of his subject—a proximity which we suspect was denied Dante, who we must presume only visited Satan in his imagination. We can suppose that Satan himself would not be dissatisfied with the fruits of Milton's labours.

There remain several issues which *Paradise Lost* does not resolve. Most obviously, Milton's cosmography begs the question as to whether other Worlds might exist, within or beyond the starry universe. The vexed question of the origin of Sin remains problematic—Milton's narrative simply shifts the origin of sin to Satan, but without explaining whence or from whom Satan acquired it. The need for gardening in Paradise before the Fall remains enigmatic. Perhaps most disturbingly, Milton makes no mention of a human presence in Heaven or Hell. In each case, it is not known if these things remained hidden to Milton, or if Milton knew the horrific truth but suppressed it.

As a matter of fact, we know that not all of Milton's epic is true. There always seemed to be a degree of dissembling; a suspicion of obfuscation; an unexpected flaw in the divine substance of the story, betraying a human hand in its fabrication; bluff and counter bluff between the various hidden hands that fashioned the warp and weft of the story.

We do know that the author and the publisher openly agonised over whether to believe the testimony of Satan—or the unseen person representing himself as Satan to Milton. But like many before and since, they had never once thought to doubt the words of the angels—or the unseen persons representing themselves as angels. Unseen, at least by Milton; if not the scribe who wrote it all down.

Paradise Fucked

He shuts and double locks the door of his flat, heads along the grubby, half-lit corridor, enters the rickety lift, and plunges down thirty storeys to the world below.

He exits to a wasteland of mud and puddles, and a whirlwind of dirt and grit round the base of the tower block. A thrawn, wild-eyed guy, in a tattered leather jacket, he trudges along the wretched road, head down bent against the weather, and the rain's getting down the back of his neck, and there is a teeth of a gale in his face and he feels as if the very elements are against him.

Man walks the blasted earth, and curses his lot, moaning and whingeing; the world's first crabbit, greetin'-faced bastard.

And he trudges to the bus stop, through a landscape seemingly forever unfinished, imperfect. Past the ragged patches of municipal grass, past a few skeletal trees, their gnarled branches struggling up towards a glowering lowering filthy grey ceiling of clouds, like a surrealist's painting of the sky of Hell on a bad day.

All around loom the ghostly hulks of slab blocks, dank and rancid dumps, doomed to be demolished, just like the tenement slums demolished before them, a wretched testament to the city's self-harm. And to think they used to call this a dear green place.

Aye right, but it's well and truly fucked now.

This wizened little man, with a wild look in his eyes, set in a creased, leathery face, complexion darker than one might imagine for one who lurks for so much of his life in a windowless bar or bookies, or at home in the top floor of a thirty-storey high rise, alone in front of his late night telly, the lights turned out and just the ghostly flickering glow of the cathode ray tube for company.

So here he is: the first one here, so he was, in the tall flats, when everything was new. He's the longest resident, doggedest, sourest-faced auld cunt on the estate. He lives alone, on the welfare, practically estranged from his family, an exile from his own past.

After what seems like an eternity, a lugubrious, dirt-encrusted bus finally lurches up and he gets on. The engine growls and judders as he slumps down in a seat and stares out the window. It's never his favourite journey this, to the clinic; something he's always glad to get over with. The truth is, he hates any appointment, hates doing anyone's bidding, hates any brush with authority, or any sense of duty. But he has to bow to the inevitability of the human condition, resigned to the futility of existence. He looks into the distance, the hangdog demeanour of a man who has glimpsed the ultimate darkness of the world, one who bears the wound that never heals.

He gets off the bus, walks a block, and enters an ugly public building. He takes a seat in the waiting room, and waits, scratching himself, retching out coughs, and waits. All over the place are the knackered walking wounded, all these wheezing croaking half-broken people, wasted bodies and half-dead souls. You'd think it was the waiting room from Hell.

Except with Hell you'd expect, well, a bit more *zeal*; a bit more activity, maybe a bit more imagination. But here we are, abandoned, just waiting, waiting, with no-one attending, and no information; they must be trying to find the fucking forms to fill in, or it's the wrong forms, or they've lost them, or they've got his name wrong, again. The whole system fucked up, no proper order to anything, and not enough staff to handle all the punters. He wonders how many people die at any one moment, and tries to imagine the size of the queue for entering the afterlife.

Finally a nurse bustles up, all breezy, out-of-place optimism, like an angel in a morgue. She's quite attractive in her own way, with a neat pony-tail and a tight crisp blouse; but she's too fleet for him to form a lasting fantasy about her.

'And how are you today, Mister…Bell?' The nurse gives him the medicine he needs to maintain his wound, and a pitying look, saying, 'Now you take care of yourself, after all, it's the only body you've got!'

Aye, right, Ah'll use or abuse ma only body as Ah fuckin' well please.

He's long conditioned to the aches and ills of his wasted flesh; not just its apparent weaknesses, but its actual treachery: its almost vindictive ability to torture him; and the certain grim knowledge that the pain built into his body is not an unfortunate side-effect, but a deliberate intention of the design.

Besides, there are others maybe worse off. He recalls visiting his father in his decrepitude, in one of the forgotten wings of some Godforsaken hospital, a room full of ghostly old crones, poor old sods who'd lost their minds, left their lives behind, they couldn't remember who they were, never mind anyone else. At least, he thinks, it's maybe better for them, to be released from their memories, released from their very selves, the whole futility of it all. At least for them, each day of nothingness is a new day of nothingness; and no need to face the jaded wait for oblivion.

Still, he's not ready for oblivion yet. When he's done, he exits the building and gets the bus back to his own bit of town. He creaks and wheezes up to the top deck this time, and lights up a defiant fag as a pallid sunbeam crosses his face, lighting up a faint crease of a smile, a little victory for the small pleasures of existence, in a dreary, ruined world.

He almost skips off the bus and picks up the pace a bit, as he's going to the post office to pick up his giro. It's not even a proper post office, but a cramped kiosk at the back of a so-called convenience store. He grumbles in the queue, impatient, always impatient, grinding his teeth in frustration at any sort of delay—and nearly foaming at the mouth when there is any chance of being cheated in the queue. He takes the cash with his usual mixture of relief and contempt. The state handouts, you are dependent on, you're supposed to feel grateful for. The paltry pittances in what should have been a world of plenty.

Next up is the bookies, where he puts on a couple of bets. It hardly matters which particular nags or scabby dogs are dragging their knackered arses round the God-forsaken track. It hardly even matters if he wins or loses: in the long run, you never beat the system. Anyway, it's only money. Like time and luck, money just seems to pass through his life on the way somewhere else.

'There is no God!' he declares, as his mangy hopes come second best and last.

'Aye, right,' says another disappointed punter, nearby.

'If there is a God, he's a Cunt, and we're all Fucked!'

Time for the pub. He heads along the windswept road again, towards a gaunt block of stone and grime on the horizon. It's one of those shabby little bars that used to be part of a tenement, but they knocked down everything except the pub on the corner, and there it is, a scabby little chip off the old block, still grimly clinging to the face of the earth, as if holding out gloomily while waiting for the end of the world.

The pub is grubby inside and out. The interior is full of smoke; there is a fruit machine in a corner, a TV and dartboard; and some dog-eared sofas; tables with dusty ashtrays and glasses plastered with brewery company logos. A habitat after his own heart: as culturally congealed, lived-in and worn-out as his own home.

He takes up his usual position at the bar, slowly eking out his carefully nursed pint of heavy, occasionally coughing or scratching himself. He looks round at the people in the bar as if looking for something new to turn up. But it's mostly the same old callous, crapulous old codgers like himself. Then again there's the occasional newcomer, fresh blood, who has somehow washed up here. He sees a youth, a stereotypically ugly, pus-faced specimen, with a grizzly dog, trying to come on to this half-young, half-good-looking woman, who has a curly bitch with her. The guy's sniffing around her; the dog is talking dog to the bitch, thinking doggy thoughts.

And he thinks of the first man, so wilfully, contrarily alone. Not Good.

No, God's company wasn't good enough for him. So, after God, he tries it on with all the animals, one newly formed creature after another. But for one reason or another, none could give the man any satisfaction.

So God split the miserable cunt in two so he could go shag his other half.

And there in front of him is his favourite barmaid— nice enough, plain face, a bit awkward and gangly. Of a certain age, young enough to be his daughter, at least. She's wearing a simple top, whose low-cut neckline displays a wilful plunge of cleavage; and plain dark jeans, whose low-slung fit reveals a wanton parting of buttocks. He looks her over and registers the imperfections—the scabs and tell-tale scars still visible on her wrists. But there's something sexy about her too: that gallus, dare-you-to-try attitude that sparks so attractively off a rough but ready body.

She's rinsing glasses and putting them away. And as she reaches up to the shelf above the bar, he thinks of the first woman, doing the garden, perfectly naked, bending over to tend the plants, or stretching up on her hind legs, calf muscles taut, and full, ripe breasts pressing against petal and tendril as she reaches up to pluck some succulent fruit from a bountiful branch.

And he thinks wistfully of that innocent age, when everything was new, and bodies were joyful discoveries, and no organ was too naughty, nor orifice unholy, for probing or pleasuring, and all manner of dirty fucking things could be done—though nothing would be so pure and dirty as the first fuck.

'Ya *cunt*!' A loud rasping roar comes out from someone at the other end of the bar. 'Ya filthy fucking cheating cunts!'

He's bitterly venting his fury and despair at the telly, which is showing a live feed of football news. A late, debatable goal has just ended the hopes of the national team, which has just endured a nerve-jangling, brave, inglorious defeat.

'We're well and truly fucked now,' says the barman with familiar resignation.

'Aye, that's everything's pretty fucked now, eh?' The old guy smacks his lips sourly as he puts his pint of heavy down.

Then it's the news; same old fucking story. Something about the car-crash collapse of the markets, and financial ruin. There's some endless war on, all going wrong. And the rest of the usual petty vices in the local news: cheatin' and stealin', violence and crime; same as it ever was, worse now than then.

'Aye, the whole world's fucked,' ventures the barmaid, like an off-duty philosopher.

'Always has been,' agrees the barman.

And God created Paradise, but now everything's fucked.

'Aye, and what's fucked cannae be unfucked,' says the old man.

Here is a man who feels a certain grim satisfaction in the fallen state of the world, a world grimly at one with itself, and him at one in it.

The guy turns back to his pint, and resumes his not-so-covert ogling of the barmaid going about her business in front of his gaze.

'And God Created Woman,' he says under his breath, as she passes, but just enough for her to hear.

'Aye, right enough,' she says; then a quiet word in his ear: 'Not then, not ever. Just so you know.'

She turns his back on him then.

And she's bending down now, fussing with the floor, haunches flexing; and he can see a naked inch of her back exposed. And that inch is enough for him to get a seedy fantasy going.

Now, he pictures her naked, down on all fours, exposing her hindquarters, and the dark drooling gash of her man-eating front-bottom, as if daring him to do his worst. But in his fantasy, the best he can manage is holding his aim over her bare-naked back, holding and— Naw, he can't quite bring himself off, never mind satisfy the mistress of his humiliation.

But then it's her turn on top, and he gets an eyeful of hairy pie as she clamps her clammy thighs round his expectant head; as her moist luscious bush brushes over his drunken nostrils, she poises herself, pursing her pungent parts—then unleashes a hot yeasty stream of piss, squirting and squishing gratefully all over his face.

He licks his lips, drains his pint, and disappears into the toilet.

And from somewhere out of sight there is a wheezing and straining tugging and then this rasping gasping groan, and there inside is the man, trousers round his ankles, and dangling down flaccid before him, the very image of God's scrawny cock and bollocks. But he's proud and defiant in the grim satisfaction that however imperfect and impotent he may be, he is fashioned after an imperfect and impotent God.

The man exits to the street, and off he goes again, trudging back home once more, bent against the wind, against the world.

And great spits and gobs of rain start falling, and it's now gushing down, as if God Himself is having an almighty Piss, soaking and mocking the Earth, making a latrine of all Creation.

And he spots ahead some teenagers, the feckless younger generation, the unwitting descendants of the bedraggled cast of survivors from a failed world. The LORD God, so mean or miscalculating or lacking in imagination, created a world too small for a runaway reproductive strategy. Like a shipwrecked orgy on a desert island, the creatures of the young Earth just can't get enough sex, just can't stop themselves fucking over the whole planet, so fruitfully multiplied they have to start killing and eating each other.

And the delinquent kids are listless, some eating gross greasy meat kebabs with their filthy fingers, others swigging spirits, off their faces on alcohol and who knows what else, howling and guffawing, laughing desperate, unhappy laughs.

Then they spot the old geyser and they start cat-calling him, and taunting him—*Paedo! Paedo! Ya filthy motherfucker!*—but he ignores them, inured to a seeming eternity of injury and insults—*Away home, ya sheep-shagging bastard!*—After all, he's been there, heard them all before.

A bit of a fucking over-reaction. Ah only ever so much as looked at her.

Soon enough, he's clear of them. He makes it back to his tower block, picking his way past broken bottles, burnt out tyres, fag-packets and johnny-bags.

Welcome home, son.

To think he's supposed to be grateful for this place, as if he should be happy just to be here at all. As he ascends once more in the rickety lift, he thinks of the broken world all around him, and the utter futility of his shitty existence, and all the despair and woes of the world. And he thinks back once more how it came to be this way.

At first, he blamed his jealous, murderous brother. Then he blamed their ill-starred, unhinged parents. Then he blamed his whole twisted, fucked-up family, its mixed-up litter of half-sons and half-daughters, the squabbling bastard offspring of desperately serviced sisters, mothers and daughters.

At times he even blamed himself.

But in the end all the roads of blame led, sooner or later, back to God, Who created everything in the first place.

Who *fucked up* everything in the first place.

A flawed God, Who'd already made His first failure—Man—with the world just a few days old. A bad God, Who gave His charges free will, then fucked them over for it. A mad God, Whose reckless command spawned an exhausted, homicidal, cannibal planet. Yes, a callous, carcass-hearted God, Who so loved His children that He was more concerned with His precious fucking tree than thinking to warn them against harming each other until it was too late. A flawed, bad, fucked-up God, Who fucked up so badly He regretted creating the world in the first place.

Aye, pal, you grind out your miserable hours—of your one and only life—in a world disdained by its own Creator. A lazy bastard cunt of a Creator Who couldn't even be arsed starting His failed world over again properly, but just fucked it over, washed it out a bit, and had another go, in the vain hope it would turn out better next time.

But all to no avail.

Look around you, pal. Paradise Just As Fucked As Ever.

High above the south side, he double-bolts the door once more behind him, shutting out the world. As he closes the curtains, the first resident looks out across the city below, a strange terrible beauty about the filthy sky and the guttering lights stretching out to the horizon, like a ghastly backlit panorama of Hell.

But it's not Hell. Far from it.

At least in Hell you'd be consoled by knowing that, somewhere, there was at least one better place. But he abandoned all hope when he arrived here, as the reality dawned on him that *this is as good as it gets*. What else can you expect from the Creator who brought you the Fucked-up Earth, but a Fucked-up Heaven?

Confessions of a Teenage Bible-Basher

It would be uncool for any teenager to admit it, but for about a year, Moses was my secret favourite author. This unexpected literary epiphany transpired just as I lurched into adolescence. With its irresistible cocktail of sex, violence and science fiction, the Old Testament was my unlikely gateway to adult literature.

As a kid, growing up wild and free on a small island off the west of Scotland, I was never exposed much to religion. My mum thought Jesus was a good man, in moderation, but not a god. My dad tended to see the Bible through the prism of literature; the nearest he got to religion was in his night school parodies of Bunyan and Milton, which said as much about the state of England as the kingdom of God.

I suppose there *was* primary school. But unlike other school subjects, which tend to progress from year to year, religious education seemed to repeat the same intellectual concepts without ever advancing—from the most corny 'God is Love' banalities to the mysteries of the Trinity, as inexplicable on the last day as the first.

What small doses of religion I was dutifully dispensed seemed limited to New Testament homilies which just seemed like a mix of common folk wisdom and literary extensions of school-room morality, but presented in quaint diction and holy period costume.

I had heard of the elder Testament, of course. But in my childhood naivety, I'd vaguely imagined it to be an earlier, out of date edition of the New version, like an old car manual or road atlas: a once sound but now superseded and not wholly reliable resource, only pressed into service if you had nothing else to go on.

And of course I knew bits of it second or third hand—the creation of the Earth; Adam and Eve; The Ten Commandments; and Joseph and His Multi-Coloured Dreamcoat (well, it was the Seventies). But it no more occurred to me to check these out in Scripture than it would to look up the Holy Trinity, the Pearly Gates or Circles of Hell—none of which, it transpires, are actually in the Bible.

Not that there was much childish demand for such kinds of religious offering on our part, as we lived our ordinary young lives to the full, living for the moment: summers playing with friends and dogs, running wild on the beach or in the hills. We simply had no use for the kinds of creation story, moral code or afterlife assurance that adults seem to appreciate things like Testaments for supplying.

Now around the time I reached the age for going to secondary school, my parents decided we'd move to

Glasgow. So, from my idyllic island home we moved to the big city, a middle-brow area of the South Side.

That first summer, alone and impatient to grow up, I went wandering around this strange new landscape, to me very urban and gritty, tenements extending in all directions, from the sandstone canyons of the inner city to the windswept escarpments of housing estates on the periphery.

Once at secondary school, I made friends with a guy called Simon. At first we talked about all the normal boys' stuff—railways, space travel, heavy metal and girls—the latter branch of knowledge spurring an unexpected sideways entry into a religious education I'd never had.

In a chance conversation about religion, Simon started telling lurid stories from the Torah, or Hebrew Bible. Of course, it soon dawned on me that he was talking about what we knew as the Old Testament. That weekend, I found myself scouring the house and attic where, among a treasure trove of my parents' old notebooks and manuscripts and boxes of my late grandfather's stuff, by the illumination of a naked light bulb in the darkness, I found a copy of the Good Book.

And my eyes were opened.

~~~

Here were all the sensational things a teenage boy might be interested in, which my previous diet of edifying literature had been lacking: wars, and slaying and smitings, and all sorts of cruel and unusual punishments. Pages and pages of the stuff. The horror of people being put to death, torn to pieces and eaten alive by lions, being hanged on trees, being torn limb from limb by a mob, or shoved into a fiery furnace. Charred carcasses and bones rising up like living skeletons, and eating flesh and cannibalism and abominable abodes of human sacrifice. Blood-curdling warlords sacking cities, putting their enemies to the sword, while maybe sparing the virgins, for personal use. Genocide and enslavement were the order of the day. And half the time this was by God himself!

God in those days was, it seems, if not actually a despotic psychopath, a bit of a teenager: still trying out the strength of himself against the world, coming to terms with his own power. Sometimes doing good, sometimes acting in mysterious ways, and sometimes doing whatever the bloody hell he liked.

And then there were the stonings, the beatings and flayings, the clapping in irons and chains, and torching whole cities, burning them to the ground. There was the story about a fornicating couple being skewered in the act with a javelin, and a tribe avenging a rape by persuading the men of the offending gang to be circumcised, and then while their tender parts were still recovering, they went back and butchered them in their beds.

Just the kind of thing no holy book should be without.

But it was not just about violence. The schoolboy imagination was duly fired by detailed instructions on the building of arks and temple complexes. Then there was the whole exotic geography of the Holy Land, the deserts, wildernesses, vineyards and mountains, smoking volcanos and salty seas; and of course the Cities of the Plain and the Rivers of Babylon. There were sea monsters, and mariners being swallowed by whales; carnivorous child-eating bears, and blood-licking dogs. Also monstrous beasts—Leviathans and Behemoths: who needed Dungeons and Dragons with this stuff? And floods and earthquakes and hurricanes and pestilence. And of course the proverbial plagues of locusts, the legendary fire and brimstone destroying cities of baddies.

And a whole range of exotic characters as you could hope to find in any fantasy novel—giants and dwarves, pharaohs and slave-girls, pimps and temple-prostitutes, sorcerers and wizards—that no-one ever told you about in school.

And then there were the remarkable sci-fi Cherubim hovering like hallucinatory vultures, speaking to the fevered minds of men in the burning heat of the wilderness, or fiery chariots blasting rocket-style across the heavens, and Elijah on board, the first primate in space. There were also the Nephilim, giant angels or angel giants, stalking the land in hot pursuit of human females. This was better than Blake's Seven.

And then you discover the dirty bits!

First you find just hints of sexual activities and capacities, with scattered references to nakedness and lewdness, then disembodied teats and foreskins and testicles out of context, and the unclean seed of men.

Then it was down to the business of sex. Not just homely old knowing, begetting, marital-intercourse sex, but real raw lusting aching grinding sex, in all its needy, panting permutations: fornication, onanism, incest, sodomy and bestiality; with a chorus of whores and harlots and temple dogs and catamites. And to think that this wicked cocktail of erotica was not some exclusively rationed, X-rated esoterica, but the stuff of compulsory curricula for God's children, fervently curated, collated, packaged, copied and distributed up the aisles and pews of churches and synagogues all over the land.

Simon had already tipped me off about the best bits and we compared notes—since the different biblical translations had slightly different naughty words, and sometimes extra dirty passages.

A particular favourite was the story of the whoredoms and harlotries of Aholah and Aholibah, sisterly comrades-in-sin who became for us sort of talismanic martyrs to free love.

Yes, I know—that is, I know *now*—the passages were all just some sort of extended allegory about religious fidelity; but at the time it was practically porn in our hands.

Here was a lurid fascination with God ranting and raving about pressed breasts and the handling of virgin bosoms. Now, I had had no inkling before then that the LORD God—who could have had anything whatsoever that He desired—had such an interest in virgin breasts. Whereas, from my admittedly partial point of view, as a pubescent kid in a co-educational school, I could well be surrounded by virgin breasts, though frankly there was as much chance of handling one of that particular class of *desiderata* as your common or garden breast, or harlot breast for that matter.

So anyway: God accuses this Aholah (or was it Aholibah?) of being like an open tent or something, and of lusting after men hung like donkeys and spurting like stallions. This was getting all a bit weird and allegorical and fucked-up really, and you couldn't concentrate on the young ladies in their breast-pressed lewdness in your head, because this God-voice kept banging on in the background about harlotry and abominations—while probably cracking one off Himself.

And what seemed like a bit of teenage kicks—a bit of a-fondling and a-fumbling of those presumably soon-not-to-be so very virgin breasts, God the big spoilsport has to ruin everything by stopping it all, by stoning them with stones and cutting them with swords and burning them with fire.

But the sexual urge is not to be so easily denied by such a literary setback. I was quite proud to finally find for myself a story with a reasonably satisfying lust content that I was able to share with Simon. It tells a tale of a young man walking around the streets of an unknown city—finally someone a bit like me, as I imagined a gangling youth treading the main drag of Pollokshaws Road. Anyway: so he meets this lady of the night, and she seizes and kisses him, and she tells him she has spread her couch with coverings and her bed with aloe and cinnamon, and says 'Come, let us take our fill of love until the morning.'

In my teenage bedroom, with no whores of my own, I imagined a sultry maiden (well, sultry whore, I suppose), with a veil half revealing her face with long dark eyelashes and sparkling eyes, and figure-hugging clothes that revealed as much as they concealed of her adult female form in as much intimate detail as my teenage imagination could muster. Though in the vision, there kept forming, unbidden, the face and figure of Simon's sister, who I was at the time trying not to have a crush on.

The point is that this ancient ration of harlotry was, sad to say, more or less my introduction to the literature of adult womanhood. Though in the story, the fill of love doesn't last very long, and the seductive atmosphere is spoiled a bit later on when it says that the lady's house is the way to Sheol, descending to the chambers of death.

Another unexpected bonus for my balance of trade in carnal knowledge with Simon was the discovery of Lot and his daughters sorting out the continuance of their dynasty in-house, in the absence of Mrs Lot (who, it will be recalled, was turned into an overdose of salt). I imagined the Lots slumming it somewhere in some

Godforsaken housing estate, where you could imagine you'd just missed the end of the world; and you were the only humans left, a single parent family on the dole, fag packets and pizza boxes and empty bottles of ginger lying around, Dad in a sweaty vest, gone to seed, nothing to live for, knocking back the beers, watching the telly; and the young ladies, ever so cool and poised but visibly bored and pacing about the place like caged lionesses, reckoning they can get their benefits paid and a subsidised flat on the welfare if they have a kid, so they ply the old man with booze, and get the old sod sozzled, then hitch up their skirts and somehow manage to get the dirty old man a hard-on just enough to get them both up the proverbial, pentateuchal duff.

And what about naughty old Solomon, the king of bling with his entourage of exotic wives and concubines and irresistibly filthy foreign gods and goddesses—which were also somehow concerned with sex, but I'll bet he couldn't fully enjoy his fill either, with the tiresome drone of Yahweh hectoring all and sundry about the iniquity of false idols in the background all the time.

But for the ultimate anti-hero, who better than Satan—who I could identify as a classic gallus Glasgow guy, swaggering around and about in the world and going to and fro upon it. He had an irresistible allure: I loved the idea of this sinewy, sweaty, russet-skinned beast, with shadowy wings, and hoofs.

Although no doubt wicked and scary if you actually met him in real life, and a thoroughly unsuitable role model, he had a sort of teenage rebellion about him; he seemed to come with a sort of self-generated power, independent of God. He may be a sinner, but he was his own man—a bit like some tough guy who gets expelled from school and you see him out on the streets doing his own thing, with the men of the world. A more potent role model, for a teenage male, than any amount of shepherds or wise men, and cooler than any super-human would-be super-hero.

It was literature and biography, history and geography, theology and science fiction thrown into one; forty-odd books of closely packed prose and verse, and finally, after all the bile and rage, the Old Testament ends, fittingly enough, with a curse.

~~~

And so what an impression it had on me, like the first gritty adult fiction you read, as if all you had ever before was like boring old New Testament daytime TV, kitchen sink dramas about parochial social snobberies about money-lenders and tax collectors, careers as scribes and Pharisees; middle-aged concerns about catering with sufficient fish and bakery products—cosy quotidian stuff befitting a small-town childhood, or a washed-up suburban mid-life rut for that matter.

But the Old Testament had gripped my imagination just as I moved to the city. It seemed in some way to chime with my wandering the streets and wildernesses, imagining all sorts of vice, drinking, adultery, whoring, cursing; stuff about how the world really, apparently, is. I learned more about the dark place that is the adult psyche in that single work than in any I had read before or since.

My adolescent biblical phase wasn't to last, however; and burnt itself out within a year. We had started to learn Latin and Greek, whose adult literature had much richer pickings. Our classics teacher circulated parodies of his favourite writer Lucian that gave us a lifelong love for 'pagan' literature, from politics to religion, and satire to science fiction. But soon enough, literature itself would be eclipsed by the dark glamour of the cinema and its domestic accomplice the video, pending actual contact with the enduring mysteries of full-grown women.

For years, my only contact with the Bible was in hotel rooms which supplied copies of the Good Book; where, eschewing the tedious ubiquitous TV and the endlessly restless internet, I could revisit my youth by slipping between its black covers and getting my fill of pharaohs and fiery chariots and reacquaint myself with my teenage old flames Aholah and Aholibah.

Yet, some part of me never let go of the idea of scripture as literature; the enduring art of story-telling and the persistence of the human condition. For the edgy old Adolescent Testament still can turn heads and grip minds, as it did mine, without having to be accepted as supernatural non-fiction. It still works as adult literature, after a fashion. Indeed, it almost seems designed that way, with its engrossing tales of the messy struggles of real-world humanity, without any easy resolution or happy ending.

Only someone who misunderstood it would dream of attempting a sequel.

The Riddle of the Cherubim

Standing over six feet tall, with giant outstretched wings, the life-sized statue of the Cherubim dominated the Professor's office, taking up his space, overshadowing his mood, haunting his thoughts. The Cherubim puzzled the Professor. It intrigued him, challenged him, frustrated him, mocked him. It occupied his labours late in the midnight guttering gaslight of his office in the University of Edinburgh. It kept him awake in the sky-lit dawn of his Marchmont town-house. It was an unspoken riddle that he could not get to the bottom of. One day, he thought, one day: he will discover the secret of this multifarious angel.

First making its mysterious appearance, as if out of the thin air at the gates of the Garden of Eden, the Cherubim had captivated Archibald Gilhoolie since he was a young child reading wide-eyed the first few pages of the Bible. The creature was a recurring subject of his childish questions, testing the patience of his teachers and trying the pious imagination of pastors. But the secret of the provenance of the Cherubim is never revealed anywhere in Scripture; and the ordinary God-fearing mortal could go to Church all his life without ever hearing of it, let alone understanding it. Now, pursuing the riddle of the Cherubim had become Professor Gilhoolie's life's work.

All scholars focus; the Professor obsessed.

Piled up and around Gilhoolie's office are books and letters, inkwells and quills; and paper, paper everywhere: over every surface are strewn seas of theses and treatises, scattered scraps of scribbled papers and notebooks full of sketches of faces, sinews and vertebrae, anatomists' engravings of horns and hands and cloven hoofs. And over and above all these normal accoutrements of the Academy are the paraphernalia more befitting a witch-doctor than the modern man of Science. Skeletons and assorted anatomical simulacra; daguerreotypes of mummies and shrunken heads; caskets of relics, racks of loose talons and wizened tendons and left-over jawbones; phials of bilious humours, musty vats of body parts, and giant bell-jars of eyeballs and pickled foreskins: the accumulated embodiments of knowledge by which he hoped to unearth the mystery of the Cherubim.

Sometimes he dreamed of Cherubim.

Fantasy Cherubim, flapping, flapping, guffawing, laughing at him. Or phantasmagorical Cherubim, looming nightmarish like birds of prey, taunting him, haunting him, with grim, baleful stares, the gaze from each of its faces bearing down on him, scaring him, searing into his psyche. He shrinks from the apparition of such a creature hovering in mid-air which must have inspired dread and awe in any who saw it from the deserts of Judæa to the plains of Babylonia.

What he obsessed about was…was…

What *was* this thing? What was it made of? How could it exist? How did it come to be such a monstrous combination of human, animal and angel? Could he detect where haunch of the lion must meet the loin of a man, or where the shoulder of the ox must meet the neck of the eagle? It was a painstaking calling, keeping track of the number and manner of limbs, tails and genitals. How many more strange appendages and hidden parts did it have? How did it come to have so many idiosyncrasies and inscrutabilities, inconsistencies and inconsequentialities?

The Professor took off his spectacles and rubbed his tiring eyes. He would pace his room and stare into the faces of the Cherubim, trying to glean meaning from each inscrutable gaze. Each countenance seemed to have a different character—majestic, indefatigable, serene, admonishing. Each face seemed to offer a different point of view. Yet it somehow added up to a single whole.

The Cherubim seemed, in its very being, a riddle.

Yet Gilhoolie was sure it was trying to tell him something.

But its silence teased him. Its serenity unsettled him. Its majesty cowed him. Its indefatigability baffled him, and finally enraged him. It just did not fit; it should not be, had no right to exist. It should not work…and yet it did. You looked at any one part of it, and it seemed to make sense, but taken as a whole, it made no sense. Or was it the other way around? Agh!

There were no avenues of the Academy that the Professor did not roam in search of inspiration or evidence. Down arid aisle and archive he sought the wisdom of Aristotle and Pliny, Bacon and Galen, Newton and Lavoisier. He wore out the wooden desks and index cards of the great Libraries. He frequented the evening meetings of the Royal Society of Edinburgh and listened patiently to the exhausting professing of learned bearded gentlemen on anthropology and palæontology. He scoured the periodicals for despatches from Batavia, or finds in Indo-China. Then he would turn inward to study everything he knew of the celestial creatures themselves: their anatomy, morphology and physiology, their æteology and physiognomy.

At night, he would awake with the sudden thought: what do angels eat? Are Cherubim carnivores or herbivores?—and how many stomachs do they have? Gilhoolie tossed and turned again in a nightmarish, nonsensical alimentary Wonderland, where cats might eat bats—or bats, cats.

And take the wings, oh the wings!

Skinny and scaly wings, hanging and dangling about his quarters; wizened waxy wings pinned on walls, or teetering from the ceiling. How many dreams and nightmares did he have of those wings: muscular reptilian wings, beating him, buffeting him; or feathered wings enveloping him, smothering him? The wings swooped and loomed over the Professor, and led him on a restless dance down new corridors of knowledge en route to fulfilling his mission.

Indeed, it was in an austere corridor of the University that the first real breakthrough came, when Gilhoolie bumped into a certain Professor Stalker, whose controversial *Morphological Taxonomy of Angels* arranged his celestial subjects, not by their theological rank, but by the number of their wings. The Professor had a niggling inkling that there might be a significance in those different numbers of wings, but he could not yet put his finger on it.

Accordingly, models and drawings of these cœlestial creatures, and diagrams of taxonomic structures started to invade the private study of the Professor's town-house. He started to piece together his notes, fixing paper scrap to paper screed, writing and rewriting and overwriting, assembling a foolscap manuscript treatise of his own…

Next, the biological, physiological, indeed physical nature of angels must be answered. If the latest theories of the universal vacuum are to be believed, then how could angels fly through such an empty medium, celestial spirits vainly flapping in airless space? Or, if angels have wings, does this mean that there is air extending all the way up to the heavens? Otherwise, why should angels need wings?

Gilhoolie found a clue in the work of an obscure philosopher, Quinn, who had published a short but influential *Bio-Physical Theory of Angels*. Therein Quinn argued that angels must need to be equipped both for travel in the heavens and in the vicinity of Earth. In the latter case, it is natural for the angels to use earthly means of locomotion, that is to say, the beating of wings in air. Indeed, a similar argument, he propounded, could be extended to the respiratory system—which is why angels have noses, mouths and, by inference, lungs. Interesting!

Back in Marchmont, the Professor's study had now become overwhelmed by notes and books on chemical composition of the air, treatises on the æther, and the latest theories of dephlostigonated air. Gilhoolie's home study was no less cluttered with the paraphernalia of the Academy than his office at the University, but included items of a more personal nature, arranged—if that be the correct word—with if anything greater idiosyncrasy than his office. Here the subject matter was even more promiscuously miscellaneous: travel guides to the Indies—the *Voyage of Bougainville*—notes on Shelley and Babbage—essays on voodoo and vampirism—the prospects for pneumatic railways.

But here, the hand of time had had more of a chance to work; as the papers had been able to settle, as if over geological time, so that Gilhoolie could locate with reasonable precision an item according to its age by the depths to which he needed to rummage. This would go back through the spidery scribbles of his university studies, his high school notebooks and ink exercise jotters, to his reverently preserved childish sketches of fantastic menageries of feathered animals and monstrous birds from his drawings at Sunday school. Even the garish doodles of the kindergarten betrayed a hint of hybrid humans that had so disturbed his governess.

Over three candle-lit winters, Gilhoolie had the physical and taxonomic and morphological features of the Cherubim in hand; but he was still none the wiser of its provenance. The professor paced his room, went out, came back, took off his spectacles, put them back on again, and stared once more at his monstrous statue. He still had to reconcile how such a creature came to be…

And then one evening at the Royal Society of Edinburgh, when he was supposed to be preparing a lecture of his own, the Professor learnt of the work of a certain Charles Darwin, whose astonishing hypothesis suggested that all living things were connected in a single family tree; and that the morphology of creatures, their taxonomy, genealogy and evolution were all linked!

And if this were true for mortal creatures, why not for angels?

In other words, could the morphological and phylogenetic characteristics of angels be explained through angels having *evolved*?

Soon, flapping scraps of paper were spreading beyond the professor's writing desk and started invading his wife's half of their study.

However, this led to more troubling questions. Does Darwin's theory of descent with modification by natural selection apply in the celestial realm? And would this imply the shocking prospect of both Sexual Reproduction and Death in the Heavens? And besides, if angels evolved, what did they evolve *from*? The Professor paced around his office, looking once more into the faces of the Cherubim…and into a pair of familiar-looking eyes.

A human gaze was glaring back at him, an answer staring him in the face.

Of course! He had been so obsessed with the Cherubim that he had not noticed that *any* angelic face is indeed, normally, a human face. This begged the question as to whether angels and humans are directly related, biologically.

Did angels beget humans, or humans angels?

It is plausible that humans are degenerate forms of angels. Perhaps the first man and woman had wings, but these were among the privileged limbs confiscated at the Fall. But then, paleontological study has thrown up no evidence of humans' ancestors having wings. So this tended to tilt things in the other direction: angels could have evolved from humans!

This audacious hypothesis would imply that humans existed before the angels; implying that Man was not God's final creation, but that the angels were. Angels, then, must be the climax of creation, and judiciously given dominion over all the creeping, crawling *and walking and talking* mortal creatures of the Earth!

Gilhoolie felt thrilled and humbled and challenged all at the same time.

And the clues were of course already there, in the wings. Seen from Earth, wings are æry, and angels celestial, but seen from the heavens, air is heavy matter in touch with the base earth, and angels in contact with mortal flesh. In this sense, the possession of wings can be seen as indication of the *terrestrial* origin of angels.

The Professor's longhand screeds of notes started spilling out once more, like never before. If angels evolved from humans, then their wings must have evolved separately from the shoulder blades, and not from limbs, as was the case with birds…The Professor's lines of argument became more tangled and tortuous, his inky perambulations looping round and back on themselves, wrapping complexity upon convolution, and convolution upon complication.

But, this could not be the whole picture. Gilhoolie's theory so far could explain angel-headed human hybrids; but not the Cherubim. He paced round the enigmatic statue, again, staring in turn into the eyes of the eagle, then the ox, then the lion. How could such a melange come about? What sort of tangled menagerie spawned such a monster?

And as images of hot-breathed bestial couplings flooded unbidden into his head in a troubled slumber, the Professor was reminded of the monstrous forms of pagan divinities: the extinct Gods and Goddesses of ancient Ægypt, lately described by a certain James McBridie of the Glasgow Philosophical Society.

And so, Gilhoolie hot-footed it over to the Library once more, and retrieved McBridie's celebrated illustrated taxonomy of deities. He pored through the meticulously crafted categories: Gods, Goddesses and Hermaphrodites; human, animal and hybrid forms.

Accordingly, lithographs of crocodile jaws and beetle carapaces, and vats of pickled ox-tails and ass-testicles started appearing in Gilhoolie's office; books and papers on the outlandish pantheon of Ægyptian and Asiatic deities now filled most of the Professor's town-house (Mrs Gilhoolie tolerated her husband's Cherubic obsession as far as the parlour, but would not allow his pagan fancies into the bedroom).

McBridie's single reference to the Cherubim is in a footnote, remarking its semblance to the winged sphinxes of Assyria and Phœnicia. A sphinx has the head of a man or woman, and the body of a lion or lioness. So a *winged* sphinx is… (he turned the page)… a cross between *Homo* and *Leo*, with wings. Such hybrid creatures—as McBridie argues—could have descended from the gross sexual union of minotaurs and griffins—unions that, in the early Earth, must have been fertile.

And it struck Gilhoolie that the Cherubim could have *evolved* from the very same combination, the winged sphinx of Assyria or Phœnicia! Zoologically speaking, if Cherubim are evolved from winged sphinxes, then this implied the smooth transition from an already six-limbed creature, where there is a simply explicable, single-stepped transition from a creature with four legs and two wings to one with two legs, two arms and two wings. An evolutionary path was plausible!

And everything was now falling pell-mell into place. Gilhoolie cobbled together a bit of history hither, a bit of theology thither; adding his own fervid insights, with physiognomy piled upon phylogeny, and phylogeny piled upon palaeontology, stern prose alternating with almost poetic evangelism. He had crossed a fated watershed; the narrative sprang forth from his inky headwaters and flowed unabated onto his expansive paper plains. With a deft editorial hand, the Professor carefully crafted together Stalker's morphological taxonomy, Quinn's angelic physiology, Darwin's evolutionary phylogeny and McBridie's ancestral winged sphinx. Thus did Gilhoolie's masterpiece eventually emerge, not so much a pure creation as a natural fusion and incremental accretion from once separate predecessors, woven together into a composite whole. And after forty days and forty nights, he was finally finished: Gilhoolie had fabricated his grand evolutionary theory of everything—all just to explain one extraordinary specimen.

As he slumped exhausted at his desk, the professor fell into a fitful broken slumber. As he slumbered, the stooping six-foot Cherubim with outstretched wings whispered in the Professor's ear, finally revealing the secret of the riddle he had puzzled over all those years.

And what the Cherubim intimated was that it was neither a purely celestial invention—a special creation, set apart from earthly genera—nor an arbitrarily fabricated human fiction; but a product of cultural evolution, descended in historical times from winged sphinxes that had real-life presence as part of the fabric of people's lives, on worn stone plinths and in dirty temples. The very thought was eye-opening. As long as the Cherubim only existed half-hidden in the pages of scripture, it could remain just a literary character. But now it could be seen as an evolved product of the world around us, it seemed much more real, much closer to us, much more credible in its actual historical circumstance and real geographical hinterland.

Indeed, the riddle of the provenance of the Cherubim was the secret of the provenance of the whole Bible itself: that it was not a special artifice of purely divine origin, but a composite creature of descent with modification through successive writing, redaction and selection by human hand, in real places in historical time.

On awakening, with freshly opened eyes, and a childish hunger, page after fresh page yielding before him, Gilhoolie found the composite, cobbled, real-world Bible finally speak its true self to him.

True Stories from Judæa

At a dinner party in Athens, in the reign of Marcus Aurelius: we find Lucian, the host, a rhetorician, historian and literary adventurer; Dorio, an old friend, a travelling merchant; Glaucus, a local citizen; Corinna, a female companion; and two intellectuals, Euandrides, a follower of the Epicurean school of philosophy, and Leontichus, who inclines to the Aristotlian tradition.

LUCIAN: Friends: I'm tired of hearing of all those hifalutin philosophers with pale complexions and long beards; of first principles and final causes; of natural theologies and empirical teleologies and atomistic cosmologies; and all those arguments about whether the world has a beginning or an end. Can't we just enjoy this evening, our food and drink, and be merry here and now?

Glaucus: But what shall we talk of, if not philosophy?

DORIO: Well, maybe it's time that Lucian told us one of his True Stories?

LEONTICHUS: Lucian? True story? You mean, like the time when he sailed out beyond the pillars of Hercules, to lands inhabited by man-eating women?

EUANDRIDES: Or the time when he flew up to the Heavens; or visited an island made of Cheese?

LUCIAN: Friends, please: in all of my travels, I always hope to report the truth, no matter how alarming or outlandish. Well, as it happens, I am ready to tell you some more True Stories: this time, from the once troublesome province of Judæa.

GLAUCUS: Well, pour us some more wine, and let's hear!

LUCIAN: Ah, Judæa…An awful place, you wouldn't like it. Well, most of it. The land is exceedingly arid, with many dusty plains. At first, it seems the desert will go on forever. Then you come to a Sea of Tar, stretching to the horizon…

DORIO: Actually, I've heard of that place. It's called Lake Asphaltitis. They say it's so full of salt and tar you can almost walk on it!

LUCIAN: It is near the sites of these two local cities, whose inhabitants were so badly behaved that their god rained down fire and brimstone and completely destroyed them.

LEONTICHUS: Well, I suppose that story could well be true. I have heard of cities being destroyed by earthquakes and volcanos... Those upheavals could have triggered combustion of the asphalt or other sulphur-based substances.

LUCIAN: Well, maybe so. But near there, it is said, a woman disobeyed her god and was turned into a pillar of salt. Can you account for that?

EUANDRIDES: Well, at the risk of bringing up philosophy again, I would maintain that all matter is made of tiny particles called atoms—

CORINNA: What are "atoms"?

EUANDRIDES: The world and everything in it is made of tiny *atoms*. They are invisible, and indivisible. *Tiny little* things. They're in constant flux, and so they collide, you see, and then they combine again with each other, in different ways, to make up all the different substances we see.

LUCIAN: I see…So in this case the little invisible atoms of *flesh* could turn into little invisible atoms of *salt*?

EUANDRIDES: Well, yes, sort of…

LUCIAN: …and perhaps pillars of salt could turn back into Sodomites?

EUAN: Look, this atomist philosophy has been developed over hundreds of years—by followers of Leucippus and Democritus…

LEON: Come, now, Euandrides. I have no doubt that your smart little atoms are theoretically plausible and philosophically sound, though as to whether they bear any relation to reality, I cannot say, since these are things that no-one can possibly see. So no-one can yet prove or disprove them!

LUCIAN: Indeed, in some other obscure part of Judæa—I forget where—I heard of a starving traveller who had to beg off a local woman, and their god supplied them with a barrel containing an inexhaustible supply of meat. So each time they went back to the barrel it had filled up with more meat, as if out of thin air.

LEON: Ah, now, that is a different matter: that is the philosophical problem of whether something can come out of nothing.

EUAN: But remember, when Democritus asserted that the world is filled with atoms, that includes atoms of air. In fact the cosmos is infinitely filled with them, circulating, colliding, combining. So it must be a case of a barrel of atoms of *air* turning into flesh.

LUCIAN: Now I also heard tell of fantastic flaming flying creatures inhabiting the wilderness of Judæa. They say these angel-like beasts have four heads and four wings and blazing eyes and coals and wheels and hover above the dusty land.

CORINNA: Awesome!

EUAN: Maybe someone needs to update the natural histories of Pliny or Aristotle.

LEON: Steady on; I hardly think Aristotle needs updating with a Lucian story. Are you sure that is a true account of things?

LUCIAN: It is, I am sure, as true as any account coming out of Judæa. Besides, didn't Pliny talk of many strange creatures, like dog-headed men, and phoenixes, which he got from Herodotus, who simply made up so much of his history?

EUAN: Well I daresay that this strange flying creature could exist…

LEON: Maybe so. But how could such a monstrous form could come into being?

EUAN: Well, natural philosophers suppose that it's quite possible for one kind of creature to change into another. This could explain the provenance of all sorts of improbable creatures.

LEON: Indeed, I seem to recall that Anaximander thought that man was first born from a kind of fish. And didn't Empedocles himself write of the ability of one creature to turn into another: of the begetting of ox-headed men and man-headed oxen?

LUCIAN: Perhaps a case of atoms of oxen mixing with atoms of men? I wonder how that could come about?

LEON: But according to *Natural History*—

EUAN:	Look, we don't need to take our knowledge from some old book. We can use our *reason*. As all things are in flux, matter may form into different compound objects. Sometimes, those may produce workable life-forms, or in other cases, they would not be viable. I'm sure the followers of Lucretius would agree that the successful combinations—like an ox-head with an ox's body—would survive and reproduce, while the less successful combinations perish, and go extinct. So we'd get a kind of progressive metamorphosis over generations of creatures...a sort of evolution, or cumulative descent with modification.
LUCIAN:	Very neat. There you see, the gallant atomist using a fabulous monster to prove his theories!
LEON:	But we don't need fabulous monsters. We can observe the process in front of our eyes. Consider: our own children are like us—yet slightly different from us; it's really not difficult to imagine that, given enough time, over the generations, people could get, say, taller or shorter, or have longer noses, and so pass those features on to the next generation.

LUCIAN: Yes and our grandchildren will have trunks like elephants, I suppose…or the wings of Cherubim. Now talking of fantastic flaming flying things, I heard a story about a holy man from Judæa who managed to fly up to the heavens in a flaming chariot!

CORINNA: Now *that* sounds pretty incredible!

EUAN: Well, it's not a matter of credibility, but of possibility. I'd suppose it's possible that a chariot harnessing some combination of fire and æther might enable a man to ascend above the earth…

LUCIAN: Æther, you say?

EUAN: Plato suggested a possible fifth element—after air, fire, water and earth—called æther, which could power the motion of the heavenly bodies.

LUCIAN: Another of your invisible substances, eh…?

LEON: OK then, how about it was propelled by some sort of steam engine?

CORINNA: What's a "steam engine"?

LEON: I'm thinking of Heron's steam-powered aeolipile, you know? But applied to propelling a chariot through the sky…

LUCIAN: Interesting…I think steam power hasn't been put to much use, other than animating statues of gods, or opening doors of temples. So perhaps this so-called steaming engine could be handy for animating flying chariots of fire?

GLAUCUS: I wonder how far our heavenly cosmonaut got to?

EUAN: Good question. I think there's good reason to believe the cosmos is *infinite*. Democritus himself asserted that there must be infinitely many worlds, some bigger and some smaller than ours; some with more suns and moons, and others without any; some with different plants and animals and so on.

CORINNA: So all sorts of things that sound fantastic, could be literally true, in some alternative world, somewhere?

EUAN: Exactly that, Corinna. In fact, the logical implication is that if the cosmos is infinite, then anything that is possible actually happens, at different times and places, and over and over again.

CORINNA: So…after all, how do we know which version of reality is true?

LUCIAN: We don't. We can't prove the existence of atoms or æther, any more than stories of fiery chariots or flaming angels.

EUAN: But Democritus—

LUCIAN: Yes, Euandrides, but according to you, *everything* can be explained by atoms, and *any* world could be true. There must be worlds made of cheese, where there are rivers of wine, and man-eating women, and steam-chariots fly in the sky, and the heavens are populated by man-headed oxen sacrificed to ox-headed gods…

DORIO: So this could imply different worlds, with different gods.

LUCIAN: Indeed, on Mount Carmel, near today's Temple of Zeus, I heard there once was a public contest between two of the local tribal gods. The priests of one of the gods (whose name, meaning the LORD, is well known; but I have forgotten it) had challenged the tribe of the other god (whose name also means the Lord, but which was a secret) to see who could get their god to light a pyre of a sacrificial ox. So the priests of the first god (whose name could be said) called on their god to light the fire, but there was no response. So a prophet of the other god mocked them, suggesting their god was asleep—or on the toilet. Then he called out to his own god (whose name could not be said) and that god answered with fire, so the ox was burned to a crisp. The crowd realised which god was the true god, and they all took to following him, except the priests of the losing god, whom they seized and tore apart, limb from limb.

GLAUCUS: And what is the moral of this story?

LUCIAN: Well, I suppose that in an infinite cosmos, both gods could prevail, but in different, alternative, parallel worlds.

DORIO: Or that different gods have different spheres of influence?

LUCIAN: Indeed, I heard of this warlord, Joshua, whose army needed more time to complete some military manoeuvre, so he commanded the sun and moon to stand still. So his god caused the heavenly bodies to cease motion, over Judæa, for a whole day!

DORIO: So this local god is trying to boss Helios around!

LUCIAN: How do you explain that away, guys?

EUAN: Well, I think this could be fitted to our latest theories of the celestial spheres.

LUCIAN: Do you mean that the Earth goes round the Sun?

LEON: I didn't realise you were an adherent of that radical, Aristarchus of Samos.

EUAN: No, no—I mean the standard cosmic model.

CORINNA: What's a "cosmic model"?

EUAN: It's the idea that the Earth is a sphere at the centre of the cosmos, enclosed within larger concentric spheres.

GLAUCUS: So all the world's a sphere?

LEON: Yes, of course. Aristotle settled that ages ago. But you don't even need to know the theory behind it. Doesn't the Earth always cast a circular shadow on the moon? You can see that with your own eyes, right here and now. See, by holding up a plate here, or a pomegranate, and seeing the different shapes of the shadows they cast.

DORIO: And surely all educated Romans—or Greeks, at least—know what any sailor knows, that the mast is the first part of the ship to be visible on the horizon.

EUAN: Of the spherical form of the Earth there can be little doubt. Didn't Eratosthenes of Cyrene calculate its circumference long ago? Well, then, it's well known by our astronomers that there are wandering stars—called planets—that normally move generally eastwards against the fixed stars, but then, on occasion, they stop in their tracks and turn back for a while, before proceeding again on their generally eastward course...

LUCIAN: Yes, so they say... by those with nothing better to do than look at the sky, or measure the moon.

EUAN: ...Now the sun, moon and planets are all believed to be lodged on translucent crystalline spheres that move round inside the outermost sphere of the fixed stars. It's the motions of these spheres relative to each other that cause the apparent retrograde motion of the celestial bodies—that some call gods—across the night sky.

CORINNA: I'm sure that sounds a very clever explanation.

LUCIAN: Ah, yes, very clever. Invisible spheres… that no-one has ever seen, let alone touched!

EUAN: Look, the retrograde motion has been shown to be mathematically possible.

LUCIAN: The fact that something is mathematically possible is hardly reassuring. You might as well say that, mathematically, things could fall upwards as well as downwards. Or that time could run backwards. I'm tempted to prefer the simpler explanation, that a god commanded the sun to stand still.

GLAUCUS: But what happened, then, to Joshua?

LEON: Did he manage to use the heavenly bodies' retrograde traverse of the crystalline spheres to his advantage?

LUCIAN: Oh, blew up the walls of Jericho with a blast from a trumpet, destroyed all the men, women and children in the city—and all the oxen, sheep and donkeys too.

They then burnt the city with fire, and all that was in it—apart from silver and gold, and articles of iron and bronze, which they kept, they said, for their god.

GLAUCUS: A case of history beings written by the victor?

LUCIAN: Or, perhaps the victor was created by the history.

CORINNA: Sometimes it's so hard to know what to believe.

LUCIAN: Just think, our beloved philosophies of atoms and celestial spheres and progressive metamorphosis could be supplanted by the simple philosophy of a sun-stopping god. Indeed, all it needs for the Judæan version of reality to prevail against a thousand years of progress in philosophy is one single leap of faith that takes their stories to be true. Friends, if I could tell stories so convincingly, I would go travelling myself, and switch to writing fiction.

Baal's Bad Dream

'Meat or bird, sir?'

'Eh, I'll have the pan-seared eagle, please.'

'Breast or leg?'

'Eh, breast please.'

'And to drink?'

'A glass of white—to go with the bird.'

'Certainly, sir,' and turning to my colleague, 'And you, sir?'

'I'll have the hand-reared meat, please.'

'Rump or gusset?'

'Gusset, please…rare, if possible.'

'Skin on? All the trimmings?'

'Yes, why not?'

'And to drink, sir?'

'The rosé, thank you.'

'Naturally, sir. We're here to please.'

Don't you just love being pampered on a flight? I especially love the long haul flights to the more exotic destinations: it really fires the imagination. The experience starts as soon as you get to the terminal, where you can see people of every colour and culture, milling around in their national dress: beautifully turned out ladies in vibrant saffron saris and exotic shimmering sarongs, mustachioed men in flowing white robes, improbably groomed bearded teenagers with hats, girls in skin-tight leopard-print T-shirts and thigh-high boots, and silver-stubbled gents in leather jackets and hotpants.

And that's just the cabin crew.

Then there's the rising anticipation, as you board, and pass through to occupy your seat, or booth, or cabin; and find all those gadgets laid out for you—a treasure trove of headphones, hand-held terminals, toys and accessories. Then you wonder who you might be sitting next to, as people squeeze into their seats, thighs strapped inches from strangers' thighs, elbows apologetically touching, and discreet sideways glances, and you wonder if you will get any of the hosts and hostesses you glimpsed on the gangway.

I love the long, overnight flights: it always feels like a bit of an adventure, those long timeless hours a blank canvas to fill as you please. You don't need to think, and the only decisions in front of you are about your own pleasure. What to eat and drink? Shall I read a book or watch a film? Shall I go to sleep, or stay up for a bit of action?

Our hostess comes round, this time soliciting our sexual preferences.

'Will you be wishing any personal cabin pleasures gentlemen? Jazz is available as soon as we've finished doing the evening meals, and we can arrange a quick boogie-woogie for you first thing in the morning.'

'Sounds great,' says Dan. 'What about rock and roll?'

'Rock and roll is only available in first class cabins, sir.'

Mile High are famed for their first-class offer: full bed, board, rock and roll, wonderful. It's expensive, though, since you have to pay for your host's or hostess's berth for the whole flight, and meals, and favours, and tips, everything. I once flew Geisha—love-hotel décor and everything—on the company. The hostess was a real honey, very professionally sexy, a class act. I hear Gigolo are good too.

'Well, have you decided, gentlemen?'

On a flight like this, I like to go with something classical from the region I'm flying through.

'I'll have the Gammon Safari, please.'

'And how would you like them, sir?'

'Straight, extra virgin, please.'

'Any particular style?'

'Whatever comes naturally.'

'*A bene placito*, excellent! And for you, sir?'

'The Caucasian Fantasy, please. One ladyboy, every which way.'

'Weiner on?'

'Absolutely!'

In a funny way I like the work flights more than holiday ones. On holiday, the flight itself can be a bit like an interruption, like a restlessly delayed gratification, when you are just impatient to get to your destination; topped with the angst of passing time when you're supposed to be enjoying yourself. Whereas, on a work trip you can relax and enjoy the flight as a journey in its own right. And, outside of certain well-defined social conventions, you are completely free from any sort of expectations or obligations. You can mingle and hang out with whoever you choose. You can just excuse yourself at any time; disappear to visit the on-board temple, or brothel, without having to explain yourself. Or just stay in your cabin seat, and have an early night, maybe watching the overnight film; you don't need to please anyone else but yourself.

I know that Dan sees the journey more as an extension of work. He looks the part: the crisp taut smart casual generation; shades, laptop, brings his own sounds; the strong, silent type, takes no shit from anyone. He's busy reading some company report, in the hope that it will pay dividends when we reach our destination. But as I see it, the flight is its own thing; you may as well enjoy it for its own sake, and all the normal home comforts that go with it. I prefer a bit of a mental break, too, while I'm in this timeless zone in the sky.

I dig out my book.

Benjamin trudges the mean streets, hands in pockets, feeling listless with guilt and frustration, trapped in this prison of society, this prison of life, the prison of his own body. All around him, the city is drab and grey, like an old TV picture. A great fog has come up, chilly and choking, its foul breath permeating the city, oppressing his senses. The citizens creep around the city, like so many sexless wingless worker-bees going through the weary paces of a dead-end life in a totalitarian hive.

All around, the glowering silhouettes of State buildings loom over him, as they loom over the whole populace, like the shadow of death. The oppressive civil infrastructure is everywhere. You can hardly walk a block without coming across some sort of physical marker of the regime of one kind or another. The pernicious Dispensaries are spread throughout the city, throughout the country, a constant reminder of the control of the State.

Every few streets, it seems, there are images of the Great Leader. He stares at you as if to say: I know what you are up to; I am watching you. And indeed, in a way he is. Not only that, the Party is. Plain clothes Party members—potential informers—could be anywhere.

Almost everyone already belongs to the Party. At least, almost everyone who counts, who expects to get anywhere within what passes for normal society. Only a few rebels and mavericks would go without Party allegiance, along with the scattered underclasses of outlaws and criminals and deviants; bedfellows too hopelessly disparate, unreliable and mutually hostile to form any threat to State hegemony.

For the State controls and patrols all aspects of public and private life. From public edicts against civil disorder and acts as trivial as urinating against walls, the State also extends its bony clutches into your own home, regulating affairs of the dining table, ablution and the bedroom. Technically, the State owns your body; it is not yours to dispose of as you wish. And most insidiously, the State aims to control your mind, tells you what you ought to think and believe. In schools, Party doctrine is instilled in children too young to know the meaning of it, the need for it, or what alternatives there might be. So everyone is shackled into an intellectual corral there is no getting out of. What's Good is by definition what the Party says; and vice versa.

Benjamin tries to look into the passing faces of his fellow citizens, to sense if they are feeling as trapped and anguished as he is. They surely can't all accept this monstrous regime. But yet they conform: not because they believe in all the propaganda, or have any meaningful allegiance to the Great Leader. They are just trapped in a historical rut they can't get out of. These unlucky citizens, born into tyranny, live out their wretched oppressed lives, lives of frustration, multiplied by wasted generation after wasted generation, with no hope of throwing off the yoke of the State—and what's worse, not even daring to dream there could be any alternative, any such a thing as a free, humane society to hope for in the first place.

But in his troubled conscience, hope is not all extinguished. He is thinking of a certain man, the one man who—

~~~

'What's that you reading, anyway?'

I show Dan the front cover, while reading out the blurb on the back: 'It's a *dystopian fantasy*, a *counterfactual allegory* and *chilling warning for society* rolled into one. It's set in the future—or is it the past?—it's all a bit strange and twisted.'

'In what way?'

'Oh, just lots of little ways…'

'Example?'

'They don't eat meat, for a start. Or pork; or even eagle.'

'So what do they eat?'

'Well, for one thing, eggs!'

'Eggs?' His face screws up.

'*Birds'* eggs!'

'Yeuch! Pass the sick bag!'

He turns back to his reports, shaking his head.

'Man, some of us have work to do…'

We settle back, me into silence, Dan behind his earphones.

The funny thing is, it's not so bizarre, when you think about it, those dietary idiosyncrasies. After all, in our society now, not everyone eats meat. Personally, I never touch the stuff. I think it's inhumane; really exploitative. It's a remnant from a barbaric past. Besides, I don't really like the taste.

Just then our hostess comes past offering us drinks.

'Do you have any fresh milk, by any chance?' I ask.

She leans over and gently cups her starboard breast so the moist nipple is within reach.

'Mmm, lovely, thanks.'

'You're welcome,' she says, smiling.

You just can't beat that warm, organic human goodness, neat from the teat.

I lean over to Dan: 'That reminds me…in this story, they drink *animals'* milk! No, really: they siphon it off, *chill* it and mix it into their *tea!*'

He winces. 'Stop, man! Enough!'

~~~

Benjamin warily approaches his local Dispensary, an ugly menacing building, built in the traditional grotesque style, from a dreary mix of mournful stone and grimacing brick. It has a gaudy billboard depicting the Party's ubiquitous geometric logo and the bearded Great

Leader beckoning to all-comers. Benjamin notes wryly that it always seems to be the most desperate, down-at-heel places where the appeals of the Great Leader seem most stridently beseeching Party engagement, promising a tomorrow better than today. Yet it's those very places which seem to have been most sorely let down by the failures of the State, over generations.

The Dispensary serves as a civic assembly hall, doctrinal school, and office of petty bureaucracy, all rolled into one. Every week the downtrodden population is supposed to report to the civic authorities, otherwise, without a good reason for absence, the Party hierarchy will become suspicious of sedition. Every week the dutifully conforming citizens shuffle meekly into the rows of hard wooden seats as if they are already in prison for some moral crime.

How Benjamin hates attendance at assembly.

It would be bad enough to have to listen passively to the eternal drivel of Party propaganda, the exhortations to be a good Citizen, and the tiresome repetitive mindless praise for the apparently faultless Great Leader. And all that masochistic death-cult stuff. Even worse is the dreary reading aloud of excerpts of the laws of the land, and case histories of notorious transgressors, accompanied by incessant threats of dire punishments, and interminable railing against the enemies of the State.

But what he finds worst of all are the participative parts—the personal submission and humiliation. You are expected to queue up and kneel before the authority of the State and declare your transgressions in the moral register. Not only is it required that you declare your transgressions, which you are assumed to have—and so it is a transgression not to declare any—but it is also a transgression to want to commit transgressions even if you don't actually carry them out.

But still, week in and week out people go through with it. An enduringly banal reason is just to conform, to be seen to conform; because to exclude yourself is social death. Another practical reason is to be prepared in case of actual death, since legally, your body is redeemable by the State upon expiry. Even if you don't care for yourself, most people prefer to spare their family the disgrace of the State disposal of unregistered corpses.

But the most compelling reason for the weekly humiliation and ingratiation to the Party hierarchy is compliance with the Sex Police. What people want most of all is approval for a State Copulation Permit.

~~~~~

'Get this. So in this story, it's a draconian society seemingly based around the control and suppression of natural urges; state-enforced self-denial.'

Dan raises an eyebrow. 'What is "self-denial"?'

'It seems to mean deliberately denying yourself rest, eating and sex, which are the *deadly sins* called sloth, gluttony and lust...'

'Why are they called *deadly sins*? Aren't rest and eating and sex necessities of *life*?'

'I think it may be because sometimes they are capital offences.'

Dan whistles. 'Seems completely perverted.'

'I know, but the point is that it wouldn't *be* perverted to them; it only seems that way to us. Our whole idea of what is perverted comes from, you know, social or moral traditions, backed by religion. The thing is, you have to imagine here a religion which is not a celebration of humanity, the pleasures of life, eating, sleeping, having sex, drugs, or anything like that; but a religion based precisely on a negation of those very things.'

'Seems a bit far-fetched to me.'

'But here's the thing. It turns out that it *could* have been our society…The whole novel is based on imagining what would happen if history had turned out differently. Apparently it's based on some story from the Bible, when God has a duel with some rival, local god. But in this version, God sleeps in, so this other god—called *Yhwh* or something—wins. So the whole of history turns on this one crucial episode, and instead of the world being ruled by God, it's under the yoke of this Yhwh.'

'Sounds horrendous. Lucky old us. Just as well our good old God won then!'

~~~

Phineas is a tall handsome man with a neat white beard and blazing eyes. He carries an aura of authority about him, sometimes adorned with an accessory air of superiority. He is an intelligent man, a reasonable man, a sensitive and within bounds a compassionate man. But his job is to enforce the values of the Party, upholding the apparatus of State. Week in, week out, he sees the wretched assembly of citizens come in to his Dispensary of Rectitude and Redemption, to declare their pathetic roster of petty transgressions—and the occasional egregious ones.

Phineas is most acutely exercised by confessions of a sexual nature. He knows only too well the boundless depravity of humanity in all its perverted permutations; and knows equally well the necessary consequences, in the sternness of justice administered to all those succumbing to the desperate engorgements and entrapments of the flesh.

He has seen horror stricken adolescents tortured by the self-knowledge of their own defilement; fornicating lovers destroyed by guilt and fear: guilt of the sinful obstruction of conception, and fear of the consequences of lack of protection, the dread of spawning unwanted offspring, or terror of the pox that rots their overwrought carnal parts.

He has despaired over the fate of desperate young unmarried mothers who would rather commit the offence of suicide than face the disdain of society and the living wrath of the State. He has agonised over abashed, anxious housewives admitting to accepting unmentionable trespasses upon their person, acts so degrading that they are forbidden even with a copulation permit. And worst of all are the abominable couplings of afflicted men, whose perverted transgressions—against society, against humanity, against nature—would in sterner days demand the penalty of death, but which in today's more clement times mean only imprisonment, disgrace and ruin.

~~~

The silver-stubbled sky-priest in hotpants disappears behind a cabin curtain to conduct some private staccato with one of his flock. Meanwhile, the leopard-print priestess zips past with her trolley vending erotic toys, ritual stimulants and holy pleasure-enhancers.

Dan buys some devotional aphrodisiacs, a couple of ritual sphincter-ticklers and a tube of lube. 'So would the poor people of the *Yahwhoo* society not get their physical needs attended to on the plane?'

'I suppose that sleep would be permitted, but only as a necessity, on overnight flights. And food would be served, but you couldn't be seen to be enjoying it. But there would surely be no sexual services.'

'Not even a little *poco* with a hostess?'

'Especially not with a hostess. In this society hostesses are banned from soliciting altogether. All religious services and confessions are strictly speaking unconsummated. The temple staff are *virgins*.'

'So…the hostesses would be—what—frigid hags with barren teats?'

'Uh, I wouldn't put it quite so crudely. But the funny thing is, it seems their society's not completely against sex; I think they're just really mixed up and masochistic about it, and in denial of their masochism.'

'So, really fucked up, then.'

'Yeah, but you know, I'd guess the hostesses would be nice enough, but you'd only be allowed to look, and maybe flirt, but not touch.'

'Ooh, torture! Women, women everywhere…'

Our eyes rove round the cabin.

All I can sense is this testosterone-teeming, oestrus-oozing den of full-grown males and females of the species, pouting and prowling around the cabin, fit and ripe for it, snugly packed lunch boxes and amply racked chasses, tautly proffered hindquarters and flashes of thigh, all purpose-built to seduce and ravish, on heat for a whole flight, overnight; but then imagine everyone pretending not to notice, no-one allowed to act on it, do it, not to say it or even think it.

'Yeah, I guess it would be a bit surreal, all right. Like a society that pretends to be vegetarian, but people go around the streets with forever roving, furtive hungry eyes, looking at the plump haunches and lean flanks and tender loins of every hot-breathed animal that passes—and then going home to get their guilty meat fix in secret.'

We sit back, still trying to make sense of a counter-factual dystopia that might so easily have come about, had history turned out differently. Meanwhile our hosts and hostesses are quietly going about their noble business, dutifully putting their God-given talents to use, in age-old rituals honouring the pleasures of the LORD...

~~~

Phineas sees a familiar slender young man approach him: a callow, pious and conscientiously confessional young man whose pathetic, protracted, tortured sexual history—mostly one of lonely defilement and illicit fantasy—could fill the annals of the Sex-Police ring-binders in the Dispensary store-room thrice over, if he filed them properly as he was supposed to.

Phineas has long pondered on the rigid restraints that the State necessarily erects between men to prevent them harming themselves. A man educated in the history of religion—and self-educated in the history of sexuality—in his darker, and admittedly more shameful private moments, Phineas wonders if in some other life the supple-limbed, nimble-hipped young man before him might not have enjoyed a virtuous career serving some other god, as a temple catamite.

Benjamin is trembling gently as he kneels before the priest, feeling he is now submitting utterly before the implacable body of the State. With sad, downcast eyes, he explains haltingly that he has a new fantasy to confess, a terrible unnatural fantasy of transgression. Naturally uncomfortable in the presence of others, he feels he is putting himself at the priest's mercy like never before. But he falls silent, unable to bring himself to inform the older man of the deepest currents of his illicit desires.

With a frisson of anticipation, Phineas gently exhorts him to declare his transgression, however personal and painful it may be. He speaks without harshness, but gently and even sympathetically, for the young man's own good. After all, he says, it is always better to inform on yourself than be informed upon. And he reminds him that even to think of doing what he may now be reluctant to admit doing is already a transgression; and to think of not declaring it doubly so.

The men's eyes meet, searchingly.

A tear escapes down the face of the younger man.

~~~

'So what happens at the end of the story?' says Dan. 'Do they live unhappily ever after, or what?'

'No, it seems that it was all a bad dream. In the actual Bible story, God really wakes up on time, and wins the duel. Yhwh is vanquished; his prophet is butchered, and the worshippers all get some meat. Everyone lives happily ever after, following the way of the one true LORD.'

The cabin lights are discreetly dimmed.

In this unnatural twilight, passengers are having their fill of 'deadly sins'. Some are slumbering and snoring contentedly; others are guzzling their midnight snacks with undisguised gusto. On the cabin loungers, couples and triples are getting down to the business of the night, each finding their own rhythm: from newly met couples' hungry *accarezzévole* to the long-haul lovers' *abbandonatamente*. All around, the gentle murmuring and groaning lends a warm air of animal charm to this tiny tin can of humanity as it goes thrumming through the night sky, an age-old conviviality defiant against the chilly lonely enormity of the cosmos; and all but two of us in our masculine intimacy blissfully oblivious to how inconceivable this scene could have been, had they lived in *Baal's Bad Dream*.

~~~

Benjamin grits his teeth. He has a deathly resigned look on his face; but he manages to gather himself together. He has decided what he must do, what he must say now. He is just able to whisper his fantasy. A recurring, disgusting, illicit fantasy. An ever-elaborating, rollercoasting-out-of-control adolescent fantasy. About a vulture.

A fantasy about first falsely idolising, and then impurely slaughtering, and then defiling, and finally consuming a vulture whose carrion stomach is bloated with the soiled genital flesh of executed sexual transgressors. On the Sabbath.

Phineas gasps; but just as quickly, breathes a sigh of relief.

He asks Benjamin if there is anything else he has to declare.

Benjamin hesitates, then says no. Phineas asks if he is sure.

Benjamin says there was actually just one other thing. Another fantasy story. About a couple of men on an aeroplane.

Phineas asks him to submit it in writing.

A Steam-Age Celestial Odyssey

I

In this Age of Mechanical Wonders, we find ourselves blessed with the ability for Man to fly up to the Heavens, and visit other Worlds. And here I, Commander A. George Griffith, present to you an account of a steam-age Odyssey to Venus and Mars; in which I not only humbly divulge the advancement of aërial navigation and planetary Science, but reveal a vision of the possible fate of our human race!

Our mission was to explore the nature of the Celestial Realm such as might be attainable by mortals; to discover any other Worlds such as might exist in the Planets around us; and to establish if there lived there other intelligent Beings. In doing so I was also curious to settle certain mysteries I had found persisting in the accepted wisdom of our Cosmology, about the nature of the boundaries between the Earth and the Heavens, the planetary nature of our Worlds, and the Communion of beings furth of our own terrestrial sphere.

Inspired by the celestial adventures of Lucian, and the blazing coals and wheels of the biblical Cherubim, I had invented a machine for conveyance in space, whose aëronautical mechanics were informed by a certain Professor Gilhoolie's studies of angel breath and angel wings. Our own veritable stream-cherubim would thrust its pistons and connecting rods in a mechanical symphony of steam power, and propel our winged craft aloft through the aether. She was named the *Zetetic*, in the spirit of the quest for scientific truth.

I had resolved to travel with a company of three other aërial navigators. Professor Samuel Adamson, the eminent astronomer, would be our principal navigator. A fiery, wiry man with piercing eyes, he may have been diminutive in stature but was formidable in intellect. Adamson had not only intimate acquaintance with the star charts but had created a good many of them himself. He had a magisterial grasp of the latest theories about the trajectory of the celestial bodies that we were to visit, and the likely conditions to be found upon them.

Miss Elspeth Esther Adamson, the Professor's gamine daughter, was an amateur astronomer in her own right, and would assist in the mapping of stars and heavenly bodies. She was also a dauntless naturalist and punctilious artist, who would record and classify any living Creatures we should come across. Miss Adamson—a prodigious linguist—would also serve as our seamstress and cook.

Finally there was Mr Cruickshank, the engineer, and pilot of our Craft. A solemn, sturdily built gentleman, with a fearsome beard and 'mutton chop' sideburns, Cruickshank had long experience of aërial navigation, and solid knowledge of air currents, winds, and the flight of birds and balloons, as well as aërial steam-craft.

After many months of preparations, the great day came for us to depart. We assembled our craft on the high ground of Gilmorehill in Glasgow. The *Zetetic* was resplendent in its gleaming brass, carmine-and-cream livery, and a commodious cabin. We said our farewells to our terrestrial companions, and cut the cords that had tethered our Craft to our native Earth. Cruickshank set the great Engines roaring, shrouding our craft in a swirl of sultry steam and choking smoke…and with a great fiery fuss and combustion, we were aloft!

II

As we ascended into the sky, keeping the gibbous Moon inclined above us, we maintained a course within sight of the icy rim of our native Earth, the world's shimmering disc so magnificent to behold so far below us. We wheezed and rattled in a blaze across the sky, like a latter-day Elijah in our nineteenth-century steam-chariot, with exhilaration and not a touch of trepidation, for we had a number of fears that any mortal should find it natural to entertain.

Our first fear was physical: that of falling; of mechanical failure or explosion, or our craft losing height, and being dashed to pieces on the ground. Then, as we ascended into the thin air of the upper atmosphere, we were fearful also about being able to breathe; but Adamson assured us that we would be able to inhale the luminiferous aether that resides between the stars. And soon enough, we found that the air had given way insensibly to aether; Cruickshank switched the engines over to the ingestion of that celestial matter, and we were able to step out onto the deck of the craft, and breathe normally, with the aether, sweet and fresh to our senses.

We were also cautious about the possibility of meeting any extra-terrestrial beings, whether sentient or brutish. We were prepared for any eventuality regarding such creatures' physical bearing, and their intelligence, social manners and morals, should they possess such faculties. In any case, we each carried with us a pistol, and also travelled with a large shotgun, a rifle, a small field-canon for good measure, and a large axe. We also carried several trunks and cages for carrying home biological specimens, living or dead; as well as geological caskets for samples of rock and dust.

But there was a further, underlying trepidation, which we had hardly dared mention even to each other. We were fearful not just for our lives—after all, each of us is destined to die—but we were also concerned for our mortal souls, just in case our Expedition into the Celestial Realm was in some way transgressing the Creator's intentions. However, we held fast to the belief that it was God-given reason that had enabled us now to make our bold attempt at celestial perambulation, and that our journey was as likely to be a fulfilment of the Creator's faith in us, as a trespass upon His celestial dominions.

The stoic Cruickshank held fast to our course, and following the celestial charts of Milton, manoeuvred the *Zetetic* dextrously between the crystalline spheres and past the Sea of Jasper out into Transpicious Space. As our craft thrust upwards, we were in awe of the wonder of creation revealed in the glittering stars. Indeed, the precocious Miss Adamson soon began to notice some new stars that we had not seen before. This was reassuring proof that the Creator had with foresight provided additional lights in the sky in preparation for the eventuality that Man should ascend to the celestial Realm.

And thus we travelled through the great Void of space. The Earth soon shrank away from us, while the great glowing tapestry of the Milky Way hung like a canvas of the future before us.

III

For forty days and nights—as far as it was possible to mark time furth of our World—we flew along on our trajectory to Venus. By evening of the fortieth night, that evening star, the legendary planet of Love, loomed below us. We descended through the swirling clouds of that balmy planet, with its tropical, fragrant atmosphere. The *Zetetic* was able to negotiate lightly through the sweet pungent atmosphere and we had wonderful panoramic views of the beautiful snow-capped Venusian mountains.

Our space-craft came to rest in a beautiful meadow on the edge of a lilac-hued lake. Our spirits lifted by the felicity of the landscape, we set up camp there and then. Adamson and Cruickshank decided to rest, but Miss Adamson and I were eager for a first reconnaissance of that enchanted country.

All around us was a beautiful verdant landscape, like a preternaturally virgin land. The air was fresh and sweet. The fragrant glade seemed to be thrumming with a blissful life. We saw dainty flying insects, Venusian butterflies, and tiny hummingbirds hovering among the voluptuously petalled flowers. We heard the singing of what we took to be Venusian birds. Miss Adamson was all the while observing specimens of the Venusian flora and fauna, which she explained in her tender lilting voice. We occasionally caught a glimpse of some delicate creature like a tapir paddling in the lake, or some gentle creatures like small deer, or peccaries, gambolling in the talcum dunes. As a beautiful dusk befell the evening star, it could not have been less enchanting than the first evening on Earth!

Alone for the first time with Elspeth, this magical world indeed seemed as if it had been created especially for the two of us. I must confess that I had fallen under her spell; my heart swelled with amorous intent for my lady companion. I spontaneously declared my love to her. She returned my emotion. Casting aside our inhibitions, we disrobed bashfully, and went swimming nude in the cool pellucid waters of a lilac lake; and so refreshed, returned breathless to the bank, where we kissed, enraptured, and decided we must be married.

As we dried and dressed, we had the feeling that we were being watched, and were disturbed by a soft noise like a little gasp, and there we found revealed from behind a frond some persons unknown: Venusian beings!

These were delicate, nymph-like creatures, with alabaster skin, and what appeared to be dainty translucent wings. They were quite naked, but looked so demure and chaste that their seeming lack of sense of shame was not troubling, but rather somehow reassuring.

The Venusians looked at us with a politely restrained astonishment but grave courtesy. They made welcoming gestures, ululating in a gentle song-like speech. With her linguistic ingenuity, Elspeth made them to understand that we came from the faint evening star above them— that is, our own planet Earth. And so, having gained their confidence, they agreed to show our party round their enchanted land.

We were taken to see beautiful orchards, rippling fields of rose-coloured cereal, glades of giant ferns and purple asparagus spears, orange broccoli plants, and wild tapioca trees, and in the distance, serrated silhouettes of the beautiful Venusian mountains, like the enchanted peaks of Kwei-Lin, or Shangri-La.

Presently we saw in the distance a great shimmering city, with a great crystal-palace in the centre, and many slender towers and graceful minarets, all sparking with arcs of electric light. We were taken up into what appeared to be a fantastic crystalline dome, which was divided into many labyrinthine galleries, of translucent hexagonal cells. We found ourselves welcomed to a great banquet, as guests of honour of their Monarch.

There, some while after we had settled into our seats, the Queen of Venus herself made a stunning entrance. Flanked by a jaguar on her left and a jacaré on her right, she was completely naked except for being draped with a filigree cobweb, glistening with dewdrops like shimmering sequins in suspension over the pert convexities and delicate clefts of her regal person.

We dined on a kind of nectar, and little cakes of pollen, and sweetmeats made of some delicious substance like *halva* or honey. We spoke of many things, of our home lands and societies. Our hostess explained that they lived in a kind of ideal hereditary monarchy. The creatures that we identified as feminine were the main active members of their society, who attended to political matters, the mapping of territory, gathering of food, and such-like.

They also had males of their species, although these persons were not present at the dinner. Afterwards, we were taken to visit one of the private chambers, and there were the Venusian gentlemen, languidly chatting to each other on *chaises longues*, preening their mustachios, smoking hashish-filled water-pipes, whiling away the time playing Venusian dice and card games. When we engaged with them, we found that they were not at all indolent, as we had initially supposed, but were courteous, tender, solicitous. They explained without trace of irony or embarrassment that they were members of the Queen's harem, and it was their proud duty to service Her Majesty and sire the population of the planet.

We asked our hosts about the tameness of the creatures, as we had seen the tapirs and peccaries mingling peacefully with the jaguars and jacarés. At first the Venusians looked puzzled, but when we made them to understand that we wondered why the jaguar did not eat the tapir, or the jacaré the peccary, a look of indelicate disgust came upon their faces, as if the idea of eating another creature were distasteful or even sacrilegious. They explained that all living things were sacred creations of the Almighty Being, and it was an abomination to think of killing or eating any such creature. They only ate natural substances intended for consumption and freely given up by plants or animals themselves—such as fruits, milk or nectar. It became clear, indeed, that the incredible gentleness of the creatures we had met was not merely a superficial appearance, but denoted a world utterly at ease with itself: a world without sin; a world, indeed, which knew no death!

It seemed impossible, or at least impious, for us to remain in such a planetary Paradise, where our very presence might confound the divine plans of the universe. And so we took our leave of our gracious hosts, returned to the *Zetetic*, and with a great churning, flapping of the wings of the steam-cherubim, ascended over the Venusian sky, and took a last look back at the Eden were leaving behind, and the likes of which we would never see again.

IV

After what must have been six or seven months of steady travel, the pale russet dot that was Mars gradually opened out before us to reveal a great dusty landscape. Most of the land was a rusty red, but it was punctuated here and there by irrigated channels of dark murky water around which patchy vegetation grew. The panorama was like a melodramatic David Roberts landscape painting of Ægyptian antiquity, or one of James McBridie's aërial daguerreotype images of the Valley of the Nile.

Indeed, we were soon able to make out some magnificent pyramids fashioned from the ruby Martian rock, and hence discern signs of some great—or once-great—civilisation. As we made our descent, we could make out what appeared to be great temples hewn out of the rock, and statues of outlandish creatures, some that seemed to have the heads of jackals or crocodiles. Wary of what powerful creatures might meet us, we were certainly now very glad to have our pistols and canons with us.

Cruickshank shut off power, and as our craft, gently hissing and chuffing, skimmed the treetops, we heard some horrible screeching noises and soon realised there were some flying dinosaur-like creatures swooping ahead. But very soon there was a ferocious rustling in the vegetation near us, and we saw to our horror a monstrous carnivorous plant with gaping jaws and terrible teeth, thrashing and tearing with relish at the warm flesh of any living thing that came within its orbit. We saw one lash out and snap shut, greedily devouring whole a pterodactyl, the last trace of which we saw was a last desperate trembling in the gullet of the monstrous plant. We steered clear of the vegetation, realising that there were hungry jaws and ravenous stomachs all around us!

Cruickshank piloted the *Zetetic* towards the largest pyramid, which we could see looming on the horizon. Directly ahead was a grand ceremonial way, and immediately in front of us opened a huge clearing, which was filled with some sort of native beings!

We came down to land in the middle of a gesticulating, ululating crowd, of what we took to be the principal inhabitants of the planet. Even before we landed, we could clearly make out that the Martians were ruddy, ugly, brutish creatures. They had tentacles, like some terrible sea-monster. Or rather, imagine a man, ungainly on all fours, with belly upwards, covered in scales; with an oversized octopus for a head, with terrible tentacles and horrible slobbering mouthparts; and festooned with dreadful pendulous genitals, and a clench of sphincters trailing threads of vermiform excrement. A less robust lady than the Professor's daughter might have swooned at the sight of them, but my new fiancée managed to suppress any revulsion at the sight of the creatures, and instead set about taking sketches of them in her zoological notebook. As she was later to recall, they seemed terrible not so much for their evident brutishness, but their very semblance to monstrous people, as if degenerate beings, pitiable souls trapped in the bodies of beasts.

As soon as we clambered from our craft, we were struck by a throat-catching stench, like rotting potatoes or rancid carcasses, and the fearsome creatures instantly surrounded us, and though we were apprehensive, it was rather difficult to tell their true intentions towards us. Some were dancing wildly as if our arrival were the answer to the ghastly sorcery of some multi-tentacled rain-dance; others seemed to be prostrating themselves before us, bowing down as if worshipping us, holding gently their tentacles out to us and coyly touching our persons. Then yet others approached us with horrible expressions on their ghastly countenances, and stepped forward to fix us in their horrible clammy grasp. They took us along the processional way, lined by columns atop of which were torches of stinking burning pitch. Crowds of the horrible brutes lay along either side of this ghastly avenue, with some grisly gesticulations, some slobbering wildly with their horrid mouthparts. Unsure if they were cheering or jeering, we began to fear the worst.

We were taken into a mighty cavern where, deep underground, the creatures sought the warmth of the interior of the planet. The cavern was adorned with prodigious mural paintings, the deep ochres and russet colouring of the artwork blending in with the terracotta surfaces of the rock, and lit by orange flaming torches. We passed what seemed to be altars of some evil sorcery, where we could not help imagining disgusting acts of sacrifice taking place: places of superstition and sin, and sacrilegious offerings to bestial gods. We tried to remain sanguine and steadfast, determined to be master of our own destinies come what may, and make any escape as necessary—or at least to sacrifice ourselves bravely.

We were taken before someone who we supposed was their leader, a particularly complicated-mandibled Martian. By means of various gestures, they seemed at once to welcome us, thank us for our visit, and make us to understand that they would like to embrace us—and place us into a large bubbling cauldron.

The lead Martian reached out a tentacle as if to seize Miss Adamson; she shrank back as we protested violently; they looked baffled, and then they backed off. They repeated the attempt to seize each of us, in each case with the same effect. We reached an uneasy stalemate, and eventually Elspeth was able to make some sort of communication with them; and so we attempted to clarify our intentions.

Their leader gave a solemn bow and slobbered a little, and told us about their society. They explained that the people were wicked, and exploited and enslaved each other; rape and murder and corruption were rife. They scorched and scourged the land; water had dwindled, food became scarce; they resorted to cannibalism. The red desert was encroaching on all sides; a planetary catastrophe seemed inevitable. Their race was in danger of destroying itself. They seemed almost completely resigned to their fate. Their only hope was to pray and sacrifice to their gods, in the hope that one god at least would answer their pleas for salvation.

They made us to understand that they believed we were Redeemers from another world; metamorphosed into a mortal life-form, and that we had come to sacrifice ourselves in order to save their race. They indicated that they were preparing to make us into Soup.

We assured them that they were mistaken, and explained that we were simple mortal visitors, and were quite unable to Redeem them. We made them understand that they must wait yet longer for their own extraterrestrial metamorphic Messiah.

They calmed down after that, and invited us to explain our own circumstances. And so we told them about our Earthly home, and our travels into transpicious space, and our experience of Venus, a place of bliss without the taint of sin or death that seemed to have never suffered a Fall.

But the Martians could not accept the last part of our story; and gave us a quite different explanation of that portentous planet. Venus, they said, had once been a world as Fallen as any other—corrupt, wicked, in an almost perpetual war-like state, ruled by a succession of despotic monarchies. The planet very nearly expired in its own iniquity. Horrible cannibalistic sacrifices were made to satisfy their disgusting bloodthirsty goddesses. Bestial creatures feasted on the flesh of each other, and defiled each other in diabolical orgies of sexual depravities that would make a Martian blush.

However, our hosts told us, Venus was saved by from its self-destruction by a great planetary Redeemer. In most gracious answer to their most fervent prayers, an extra-terrestrial Messiah had metamorphosed into the form of a local Venusian horned insect-creature—born bodily as a sanctified larva of an unfertilised egg—and offered itself as a personal self-sacrifice to save the planet. The Almighty Supreme Deity then showed His infinite Love and Mercy by restoring the planet to its original condition of immortal bliss, and everyone now lived in a literal Paradise of eternal peace and harmony and plenty, as if the planet had never suffered a Fall. Such was the truly blissful state that we had indeed found so magical in Venus.

As we journeyed back across the desolate silence of space, we reflected ruefully on our own wretched, botched World, a great Ruin, so obviously still fallen, riven with sin and vice, darkness and death; where we, the wretched sons and daughters of Adam, are still sadly denied a Redeemer of our own, to restore an Earthly Eden.

Zombie Messiah 2

The first inkling that something is not quite right is when I realise that the venue isn't the small independent studio I was expecting, but one of the larger ones where they do the space movies.

There, outside one of the studio exit doors, I spot a couple of what look like long-haired locusts smoking cigarettes. And I'm thinking, what the heck. But worse, a seven-headed dragon comes ambling out of the emergency exit, chatting to the actor who is supposed to be playing *my* main character...followed by what appears to be a seven-eyed woolly mammal irritably fumbling with its smartphone. The realisation dawns that these bizarre creatures must be somehow connected with what was supposed to be *my* movie.

I can't think of how scary dragons or angry lambs could relate to the life and times of one of the world's most charismatic holy men, but given the director involved I shouldn't have been surprised at the prospect of a surreal, postmodern twist on things.

As I get closer, the first locust—who has a visibly human face—taps ash off the end of his cigarette, and gives a big grin, revealing teeth like lions' teeth.

So I ask them, straight out, what scene they're in.

'The time of the great tribulation…'

'That's not some flashback to Exodus, is it?'

'No, more of a flash forward to the end times…'

'…when we get to torture sinners,' says the second locust, pointing to her scorpion tail.

'…when the ground opens up, the dead rise, and the undead stalk the land…'

'It's the denouement of the film, don't you know it?'

~~~

A gaggle of bearded men turn to look at me when I am eventually shown into the plush editorial suite. They are evidently engrossed in discussions about the set— something about smoke rising from the Abyss and how to create the illusion of a bottomless pit.

Then one of the guys breaks the silence, and leans forward to address me. It's the producer, a smooth, waxy-skinned man in an expensive looking dark suit and bold, artistic looking tie.

'Hi, I'm Paul,' he says, grinning just a little cheesily, gesturing me to sit down. 'And this is—of course—John, the director; and these are our chief scriptwriter, production designer and art director'.

'So, how can we help you?' says the director, a vaguely dreamy looking man with a goatee beard, and a tight pony-tail, wearing an open-necked shirt and a chunky beaded necklace.

'Uh…' I clear my throat. 'I heard a rumour that you had already completed the movie, and had made quite a lot of changes from my original script.'

The producer and director look at each other, a bit shiftily, even guiltily.

'Ah yes,' says the producer. 'Now let me explain. We loved your work, but…'

'…We had to make some changes.'

'Changes?' I say. 'What kind of changes?'

'Now the thing to remember here is, this movie is going to be a *classic*. But it's mainstream classic, not cult classic, right?'

'Er, yes.'

'OK so, as I am sure you know, we had to make a few changes. First off, we cut out most of the sex and most of the politics—'

Just leaving the religion, then…? I wonder sourly.

'—and also any specific references to dates. We also changed the title, to make it more focused on the unique characteristic of the main hero.'

'You mean, that Joshua was martyred?'

'Well, yes, and no. Thing is, he doesn't die at the end any more…no. Your original ending—defeat—death—

149

etcetera—the guy's too much of a loser. For our target audiences. He must be a hero. Hollywood style. *Mainstream*. You do understand, right?'

I bite my lip.

'But…isn't that changing the whole thrust of the story? It's about a tribe, a tradition, an insurgent preacher, a prophet of peace, who dies for his cause.'

'Okay, so, it's true he dies for his cause. But you must understand, it's the bigger picture we're interested in…'

'Bigger picture?' I say. 'But, the whole future of the Judean insurrection hangs on this one man's fate!'

'Look, my dear, this motion picture; it's not about *Judea*; it's not about a few peasants in the wilderness; it's about you and me, *all* of us!' says the producer, gesturing round the table of middle-aged, besuited, bearded men nodding in unison. 'We can write this story on a bigger canvas! Think of the numbers! A movie based on one tribe, performed only in Aramaic…you'd be lucky to get it in a handful of art houses on the west coast. But this—*this*, we can get it into all the multiples, all the majors, right across America—'

'And across the globe,' says the director with a far-away look, 'Wherever there are movie theatres…'

'You know how many movie theatres there are in America?' says the producer.

'But how can you expect to—as you put it—widen its appeal?' *By adding dragons*? I'm thinking.

'By opening it up, making it global.'

'We take your man, and we give him to the world.'

'Jesus the Saviour, Redeemer of all humanity.'

'Jesus?'

'It's the Greek version of Joshua,' says the scriptwriter, pedantically.

'I know that, but what's wrong with Joshua?'

'Well…it's just a little…'

Too Jewish?

The scriptwriter speaks up again. 'It could be confused with another character called Joshua'—as if this coincidence of names were a scripting slip-up on my part.

'Anyway, Jesus is not really Jewish.'

'Not really Jewish?' I could barely contain myself. 'He was only crucified for being King of the Jews!'

'Ah, yes, but he was his own man…a new kind of Messiah…'

'He is the *Christ*. The anointed one…' says the scriptwriter, earnestly.

'He's the Son of God', says the producer, effusively.

'… and He *is* God' adds the director, enigmatically.

'Hang on there…Messiah, OK, OK…I recognise the concept—even if I don't think it applies in this case. Son of God—I get the gist, though it sounds a bit pagan. But you're saying he also somehow actually *is* God as well? How can that work, even logically, never mind theologically?'

'Trust me. It may sound a bit funny at first, but we think it'll work okay, actually.'

'But scripture just doesn't work like that. The rabbis surely wouldn't approve such a…*perversion* of Judaism…'

'Ah yes but you see, my dear, it's not Judaism any more. That's the thing. It's, like, a new religion...'

'…a new *kind* of religion, not based on a particular people in a particular place.'

'We're calling it Christianity,' says the producer, crisply.

'A new religion? But how does this all relate to my story?'

'Well, your story is very much part of it; a very important part. It supplied the main character; provided the context'—and the director waves his hand airily around him—'that set the scene, set the challenge, and so on and so forth *et cetera*; and it is all resolved in the end. By Jesus.'

'Besides,' adds the producer, a touch frostily, 'we have no agreement to stick to your story. As agreed in our contracts, we have the rights to use any of your material in our movie, and any other formats. You have the right to publish anything we don't use, as long as it doesn't interfere with this or any future version.'

'So, no unauthorised Second Comings!' says the director.

They all snigger.

Just then, an assistant looks in and says that the video suite is free, and coffee has arrived. So they deposit me in a room with a control console and large screen, and I am left alone with an unsolicited skinny latte and a *fait accompli* of a movie.

~~~

As I start to flick through the movie scenes, the first thing to notice is the change of title: where I had had *The Nazarene Martyr*, we now have *The Zombie Messiah*. I struggle to navigate the surprisingly large menu of contents. Instead of a single main feature, there are four different versions of the story of 'Jesus', apparently written by four different scriptwriters, each giving different perspectives on the same story. As if making four different versions of events made it *more*, and not less likely, for any one of them to be true. All very postmodern...

Then there is a whole bunch of 'extras', seemingly monologues by the producer, sounding like a Gazetteer of the Roman Empire. The effect is to shift attention away from the Holy Land to more glamorous locations in the west—places like Ephesus, Corinth, Rome.

As I flick through different scenes, it becomes clear that they really have taken out most of the politics and sex. They must have conveniently removed almost all references to Joshua as a red-blooded man, a fundamentalist freedom-fighter, and any mention of Jewish nationalism or the injustices of the Roman occupation—anything that would rock the boat or limit mainstream acceptance.

And they seem to have written out the intimate, formative influence of Mary Magdalene, one of Joshua's closest confidantes; or else twisted her character to suit their prejudices. Joshua is now surrounded almost completely by sturdy obsequious men, and compliant or fallen women. It seems they already have it all stitched up to fit their own agenda.

The assistant puts her head round the door. 'The director and producer have another meeting shortly. Do you have any other questions for them?'

~~~

I step back out to where the others are in discussion—about a scene involving vultures coming round for supper. I can barely contain my anger and hurt and bewilderment, but address them as coolly as I can.

'Look, I appreciate that you're just trying to make the movie more popular. But to be honest, I'm not happy with all these changes. What has happened to Joshua, and his actual cause? The whole point of my script was to get Joshua's message of love and peace out there, and his radical reinterpretation of the holy laws, to cap the rest of Hebrew scripture.'

'Yes, we thought about this,' says the producer, coldly. 'But the way you had it, he seemed to say little more than "Be good, and by the way, God's now in a better mood."'

'But Joshua's message is much more than that—his ministry is all about love, humility, forgiveness, as well as challenging authority and exposing hypocrisy. It's about giving to the poor, giving solace to the oppressed, elevating the meek and empowering the weak.'

'Yes…well…that's a bit *too* radical, I think,' says the director.

'Too much like Socialism!' quips the producer.

'Which is, er, fine, don't get me wrong,' says the director, 'for a personal philosophy. But not a model for actual political power in this world…'

'Your version put too much faith in insurrection; ours is more about *resurrection*!'

'Resurrection?'

'Well, Jesus dies on the cross, you see,' says the director, 'but *then he comes back to life*!'

'He's dead, then he's not dead,' explains the script-writer, unnecessarily.

'The best of both worlds, you might say,' adds the producer.

'Sorry, what? Comes back to life…? Like Lazarus?'

'Yes, but it's more than a biological revival. In this case Jesus actually conquers death itself!'

'For everyone!'

'So he can offer everlasting life to everyone who accepts him as Saviour!'

'Think of the audience for that, my dear. We can appeal to *everyone*!'

I consider the implications. The movie is now little to do with Joshua of Nazareth. Now, the way they've filmed it, the radical social conscience of Joshua will be forever mixed up with the hero-worship of a mythical living Christ-God-person—someone preoccupied with his own glory and special relationship with his Father.

'But besides,' says the producer, 'since Jesus comes back from the dead, it allows us to create a smashing sequel.'

'A sequel? What kind of sequel?'

'Zombie Messiah 2: Return of the Son of God.'

'It's a futuristic science fiction fantasy.'

'We thought we'd freshen things up a bit, paint things on a yet larger canvas. That's where John comes in—visionary director extraordinaire. And of course, these guys doing the storyboard and the set.'

'We're shooting right now...'

'But after a resurrection, what more is there left to happen?' I ask.

'The plot, well, it's a bit hard to summarise...,' says the producer, looking around, as if for help. 'A time of tribulation, a final battle between good and evil, destruction all around, etcetera…It really talks to our times…indeed it's for all time!'

'And the special effects are going to be fantastic!' says the director.

'We have this scene where the stars fall to Earth and the whole sky rolls up, like a scroll!' says the art director.

'And don't forget the asteroid strike!' says the production designer.

'A giant meteorite falls from the sky, like a big burny mountain crashing into the sea.'

'…annihilating a third of the sea life—and a third of the shipping on the seas!'

'And the whole ocean turns to blood…'

'Don't forget the brimstone, the giant hailstones and the lake of fire…'

And I'm thinking, what next, a cometary cataclysm that sinks Atlantis and forces an exodus from the original Holy Land?

'Oh, but it's not just the plot. We've got lots of fantastic new characters.'

'You mean, like human-headed locusts?'

'Yes, the locusts, the seven-eyed Lamb and the seven-headed dragon—you may have seen him around the set. We also have the Lion of Judah, the Beast, and the Sea Monster, and of course the Horsemen of the Apocalypse…'

I had heard of Pride and Prejudice and Zombies—I'd even seen the film—and I had heard of a sequel, Sense and Sensibility and Sea Monsters. But this was getting ridiculous. What next—The Zombie Messiah and the Seven-Headed Sea Dragon?

'But tell me,' I say, 'are there any normal people in this movie—anyone I could identify with?'

There is a thoughtful pause.

'Any women at all?'

'Well, there's the Whore of Babylon…'

'The Whore—?'

'Oh, she's symbolic,' says the director.

The art director cuts in. 'She has a golden cup in her hand, filled with abominable things and the filth of her adulteries.'

'She's drunk on the blood of the people.'

'And what does her story symbolise?'

'Oh, the ruin of Babylon.'

'So what happens?'

'They strip her naked, eat her flesh and burn her with fire.'

More silence.

'Wait, so the only female character is a cannibalised sex worker?'

'Well, there *is* also the virgin mother of God...'

That's some choice of female role models, right enough.

'But let's not forget the Return of the Son!'

'The Christ character is by now our supernatural superhero, a celestial warrior, riding on a magnificent white horse, with a great sword, leading an army of angels, and defeating all the devils and dragons, throwing them into the lake of fire where they are tormented forever and ever.'

'What more could you want from a story?'

'But Joshua was a meek and humble man. An underdog, who rode on a donkey. You lose completely his message of peace and humanity.'

'Look, to be perfectly frank, every age has charismatic preachers, every tribe has passionate martyrs; history is littered with them. But we are talking about the greatest story ever told—this is the Son of God, divinity made flesh, with the key to everlasting life!'

I have to admit that my simple human story just can't compete with that.

'Look, if it's any consolation, this happens all the time in this business—earlier characters and writers are always being upstaged and over-written by later ones. It's just part of the game.'

'Just look at the history of the Bible. I daresay those who wrote the Torah wouldn't be too pleased to see your Joshua come along and change their story, steal their thunder.'

'And who knows what or who will come after *us*?'

~~~

The assistant announces that their next appointment is here—a tall, clean-shaven guy in a dark suit—'the other writer, a Joseph something-or-other, with the proposed sequel, set in America.'

But I'm already out of there. Mentally shattered, I nearly bump into a loitering horseman of the apocalypse, as I head for the exit.

Outside, I spot Jesus slouched by the emergency door. As we share a guilty cigarette, I shed a little tear as I reflect on the wreckage of my dream.

My script has been ripped up, my hero recycled, my message eclipsed by the unhinged fantasies of John and evangelical enterprise of Paul. And so it came to pass that *The Zombie Messiah* triumphed over *The Nazarene Martyr*, and the story of the mortal Jesus was sacrificed, so that the myth of the immortal Christ might live. As my gospel of Joshua finally bit the dust, so too did my own chance of literary immortality, as the writer who originally breathed life into the legend.

'Never mind,' says Jesus, 'It's only a movie.'

Motoring in Bunyan Country

One of the special pleasures of travel is the delicious disorientation we feel when a place that we have known only in our imagination appears before us as a defiant, reckless reality. And now, as we touch down on the tarmac, the cabin crew hail our final arrival in Bunyan Country. The land immortalised by John Bunyan in Pilgrim's Progress is an obscure, once-famous-for-something sort of place, like Timbuktu or Xanadu, to which we are still drawn, according to the explorer's classic mantra: 'because it's there.'

The principal points of arrival are the airports of the big cities: the main international gateways are at Vanity and the City of Destruction. But some fly-drive packages allow you to drop off your hire car at local airports in the Country of Conceit and the Plain of Ease.

The City of Vanity is the undisputed commercial and political capital of the whole region, and is the first port of call for most visitors. It is the jewel in the crown as far as the modern tourist industry is concerned, not least due to the world-renowned Fair held there.

Vanity's Fair has a thriving trade in all sorts of merchandise. Traditionally this was precious metals and stones, but increasingly also fashion, electronics and other consumer goods. Business is brisk, with the benefits of duty-free and easy credit; but watch out for fake brands. They say that anything that can be bought and sold can be bought and sold there: from Lands to Honours, to Pleasures of all sorts—and even Bodies and Souls.

The Fair is also famous for putting on many entertainments, including plays and games. In Bunyan's day these would include chess and juggling acts; nowadays there are also casinos and virtual reality gaming arcades. With the city's fine dining establishments and trendy bars and nightspots, Vanity is an important venue on the conference circuit, with plenty of extra-curricular activities for delegates and their partners.

Although boasting all the latest brands and fashions, Vanity's Fair is actually of ancient provenance. Not many know it's over five thousand years old—and was noted for its antiquity even in Bunyan's day. The powerful families who ran the town are still by and large in control to this day, though there are always new arrivals, and powerful positions are now held by women and outsiders. Lord Desire of Vain Glory and Sir Money-love still rule the roost. Lord Carnal Delight and his mistress Lady Lechery are very much at home in town, along with newcomers Lady Petty Debauchery, her half-sister Lady Instant Celebrity, and their outrageous bedfellow the Earl of Goodly-Vibration. The main difference from Bunyan's day is that the Vanity Metropolitan Area is now a much more liberal municipality. It no longer burns Christians at the stake; in fact, prominent Christians are among those running the show.

Beyond Vanity, the other main centres of population are situated around the City of Destruction. This is a rather graceless city, whose main claim to fame is as the departure point of the hero of *Pilgrim's Progress*, on his journey of faith and redemption 'from this world to that which is to come'. The city is part of the wider Conurbation of Destruction, which also includes the Town of Carnal Policy, Wanton Garden Suburb and the Gated Community of Gratuitous Celebration. Some of these cities and towns are nice enough places to live—and the University of Carnal Policy is popular with students—but they hold little interest for the short-term visitor.

Apart from Vanity, the main attractions of Bunyan Country are in the rural hinterland. For natural landscape, the main draw is to the South, and the Delectable Mountains. Here there are many woods, vineyards, orchards, and gardens, all watered with springs and fountains. In Bunyan's day, there was sheep farming here, but today the whole area is now part of the Delectable Mountains National Park and Nature Reserve. The mountains are celebrated for their pleasant prospects, although, as with many mountainous regions, the sense of wonder is seasoned by the frisson of danger. One of the peaks, called Error, is notorious for its steep sides and cliffs strewn with the remains of incautious mountaineers, their broken bodies left unburied as a warning to others. Sticking to marked trails is strongly recommended here. There are also some subterranean passages in the area, smelling of brimstone, which by local tradition are where famous sinners such as Alexander the Great, Virgil and other blasphemers were taken directly to Hell. These passages are now closed off to the general public, on grounds of health and safety.

There is no finer way to traverse this country than by car; all the pleasures of the open road await the modern pilgrim retracing Bunyan's footsteps. In the old days, roads were bad and dangerous, but in most parts, good modern roads are the order of the day, and today's motorist hardly notices the hills and defiles that once loomed large as serious challenges for travellers.

Heading out of the City of Destruction on the King's Highway, we soon come to the Slough of Despond. This notorious bog, full of the filth and scum of sin, was a major barrier to travellers in historical times. For sixteen hundred years, as Bunyan noted, His Majesty's Surveyors had employed labourers to fix it, with twenty thousand cartloads of aggregate deposited into the quagmire in order to try to stabilise it and make a path through. This was all to no avail. It was only much later that a proper route was laid across the Slough. The Victorians first managed this by 'floating' a railway line across on top of beds of brushwood. Nowadays, a modern road crosses the Slough on a graceful bridge that clears the quagmire in a single span. (The bog itself is protected as a nature reserve, as the filth of sin is recognised as harbouring valuable biodiversity.)

One of the most challenging locations on any journey was (and is) the Valley of the Shadow of Death. The old road through this gloomy defile was a classic rite of passage for the would-be pilgrim in Bunyan's time. The valley is a wilderness land of deserts and burning pits, traps, pitfalls and deep holes. The road itself, an ancient trail, is extremely narrow, beset on one side by a ditch and on the other by a quagmire. Here the traveller must negotiate hazards including blood, bones, ashes and the mangled bodies of those who went before.

In modern times this road has proved too daunting for the general public to bear to travel through. But any attempts to improve the old road were also problematic: there were difficulties with the alignment itself, the underlying geology, and problems of disturbing the habitat of dragons and other rare but dangerous indigenous creatures.

In the end, rather than attempt to improve the old road, the King's Highway engineers decided the best solution would be to simply by-pass the Valley altogether, almost as if it did not exist, with a new modern asphalted road. But the modern visitor need not be disappointed at missing the visceral thrill of the Valley. There is also a new access road that extends as far as the lip of the abyss, where there is a viewing point, with a coach park and toilets. So the modern traveller can arrive there in comfort and get panoramic views over the phantasmagorical landscape of damnation. While the view is superb, motorists are advised to keep their windows up, to avoid exposure to the distant stench and hideous noises coming from below.

There's a good range of accommodation in the region to suit all budgets. There are decently appointed roadside inns, such as The Wicket Gate, which has free parking and a child's play area, located next to a large roundabout. For budget travellers, there are also campsites in the Delectable Mountains. At the other end of the scale, there are more sumptuous hotels, including a converted Palace called Beautiful. This contains its own museum, with some old records and religious relics, but is perhaps most famous nowadays for the Lions in its grounds. For an overnight stay with a difference, Doubting Castle is now a themed tourist attraction. Visitors can follow in the footsteps of the Pilgrims, by first being locked in the dungeons of Doubt, and then being released by the Key of Promise. Keys may be hired or bought in the castle Shop.

Our sojourn in this enchanted land would not be complete without visiting the Cross and Sepulchre. Although in Bunyan's time almost everywhere in the Country had some sort of religious significance, most of those associations are lost on the average traveller of today. Nowadays the main focus for religious attention is concentrated on the Cross. This location, now an essential stopping point for coach tour parties, is regarded as the highlight of the journey for modern pilgrims; but believers and non-believers alike will find interest in the site, if only for its historical significance. There is a small exhibition, souvenir shop, and café. Pilgrims can send home postcards franked at the local post office as a record of their piety.

The original destination of Bunyan's hero in *Pilgrim's Progress* was, of course, not the Cross itself, but the Celestial City of Everlasting Life: a radiant metropolis lying some way beyond this Country, across an unbridgeable River. According to Bunyan, this City was built of pearls and precious stones, and its streets were paved with gold. Its citizens wore crowns on their heads, held palm branches in their hands, and played on golden harps. Some had wings.

It is unlikely that Bunyan's was a first-hand account of the Celestial City. But, regardless of the exact details of the celestial etiquette and street infrastructure, the general impression of a heavenly city has proved remarkably resilient down the ages. And the existence of the Celestial City has had a lasting influence on the hearts and minds of citizens of Bunyan Country: all manner of affairs on this side of the River would simply not make sense without it.

The roads of Bunyan Country are filled with travellers of many kinds. As well as *bona fide* Pilgrims intent on passage to the Celestial City, there are Atheists, who are conscious that they are destined nowhere in particular, and know they must enjoy their journey for its own sake. But in a sense, Bunyan's original guide *Pilgrim's Progress* was always aimed with an eye to waverers: especially those settled in some comfortable suburb of the Conurbation of Destruction who harboured aspirations of gaining admittance to the Kingdom of Eternal Life, yet never attempted to hazard the journey.

And there are still more people looking for something beyond Bunyan or the organised tours. These are independent travellers trying to find their own way: they are typically sceptical about the claims made for the Celestial City; yet their outlook is still deeply shaped by what they suppose lies on the other side of the River. Some of these are pious Atheists and Agnostics who travel in hope—pilgrims despite themselves—bearing all the hazards of the road, foregoing the pleasures of Carnal Policy and delights of Vanity Fair, as if expecting some rewarding destination should await them after all.

Then there are those who, like new age travellers tiring of life on the road, finally pitch up at some Trailer Park of Procrastination, neither properly settled nor making progress anywhere else. Others try their lot with the new age pagans, squatting uncomfortably in the grounds of the Castle of Beëlzebub. Then finally there are ordinary commuters of the Conurbation of Destruction, who shuttle back and forth in their daily lives, barely giving a thought to their ultimate destination.

As my flight home ascends into the sky above the Plain of Ease, I reflect how modern travellers can now see this whole Country much better, revealed from viewpoints Bunyan could not have foreseen. Each must find their own path, and their own desired destination, and a package to suit their circumstances. As we soar over the Delectable Mountains, I look out for the Celestial City beyond the clouds.

One Thousand and One Afterlifes

A gentle zephyr plays on the leaves of the almond trees as the fragrance of incense drifts across the tranquil courtyard. The trickle of a fountain may be heard, and the quiver of a distant stringed instrument. The dark water of a courtyard pool reflects the shimmering moonlight. And in the flickering light of the royal apartments, a young woman kneels before the great Sultan. Her eyes shine like sparkling jewels, and her voice is like a melody; but her smile is melancholy. She breathes softly, but somehow more tensely now as she nears the end of her story.

The young storyteller draws her narrative to a close, and then waits.

At length, the Sultan speaks.

'Shirazad, I have been entertained by your many tales of sultans and viziers, princes and princesses, dervishes and genii, and sailors crossing the seas, and caravans crossing the desert of no return. I have also been enchanted by your fables of talking trees and serpents, mermaids and marionettes, minotaurs and griffins, cities of brass and mansions on the Moon. Yet, I am intrigued by the idea of a king who has all the riches life can offer, but who might yet be granted something beyond this life.'

'So may it please His Majesty for me to tell him this story on the morrow?'

The Sultan looks at her serenely and replies, 'Let it be so.'

And so the next day, Shirazad told this tale.

'Once upon a time there was a great king called Asahuerus, who lived in his royal palace at Shushan, and reigned over a hundred twenty and seven provinces from the shores of India to the wilderness of Ethiopia. But though he has everything a king would wish for, he is yet weary of his existence. So he calls his vizier to find him some new experience to live for.

'The vizier duly sends out emissaries across the hundred twenty and seven provinces of the King of Shushan. Soon enough, he learns of a foreign slave who is doing wonderful things, healing the sick and bringing joy to the hearts of the people.

'So the slave, whose name is Didymus, is brought to the great city of Shushan; he is led through the gates of the king's palace, and into the throne room where the king receives visitors. The doors are opened, and the vizier urges the ragged man forward into the king's presence. The newcomer prostrates himself before the king, touching his forehead on the carpet at the feet of the throne, and waits to be called.

'Then the king holds out his golden sceptre, and invites the man forward.

'And the king says to Didymus: I am tired of life. I have all that a king may possess, and I have done all that a man should wish to do. And yet, I am melancholy. I crave something more, something more than what this life offers. What can you give to me?

'And Didymus says, Sire, if it should please His Majesty, I can build you a new palace where you can live a new life. But the king says, I already have a magnificent palace. The vizier cuts in, saying, behold, the king's palace with its pillars of marble, and paving of porphyry, and alabaster and lapis lazuli; a palace with curtains of purple, and beds of gold and silver. But Didymus says, your palace is indeed magnificent. But I can build you a different kind of palace, in a verdant and well-watered place beyond the city, where the air is fresher, and where you could escape from all the cares of the city and the burdens of office and this life. The king says, can you build me such a palace? And Didymus replies: Sire, I am a carpenter and builder; I can build His Majesty a palace, and also furnish it.

'The king is pleased and asks the carpenter to prepare a plan. So Didymus draws out the layout of the summer palace, with doors facing towards the east and the light of sunrise, and windows to the west to the warm breezes, and with a bakehouse towards the south, and an aqueduct to the north. The king is delighted by the plan, and orders the carpenter to be handed bags of gold and silver, for buying materials and paying the labourers.

'And so the months pass. From time to time, the king's vizier sends out despatches asking how progress is going, and Didymus always assures the vizier that things are going well, but asks him to keep sending more gold and silver. And the time passes, for two summers, in such a manner.

'But as the next autumn chill comes, rumours start to reach the king from the region where the summer palace is to be built: of a dervish or holy man who lives a very humble simple life, but who is giving away gold and silver to widows and orphans. There are also reports of a magician or sorcerer, who is able to interpret dreams, who has been healing the sick and casting out demons, and doing other wonderful things. So the king, growing suspicious, asks some tradesmen who had been in those parts whether they had also seen—among these many wonderful things—a magnificent palace rising from the plain. But they say they have seen no such palace; nor have they seen or heard of any men hewing stone, felling trees nor crafting furnishings. The king's countenance darkens and, now full of wroth, sends his vizier to inspect the site of the palace, and bring back the carpenter to account for himself.

'And so the vizier goes to the location chosen for the palace, to find nothing but Didymus living in a hovel, among the poor, widows and orphans. The vizier has the carpenter seized and brought back to the palace in chains. He is thrown to the ground before the king, who demands of him what has he been doing?—what has the money been spent on?—where is my new palace? Didymus replies, I am building His Majesty a better palace, one not for this life, but the next…The king, now enraged, has Didymus flung into the royal dungeon. The vizier asks the king about how to deal with the disgraced carpenter.'

At this point, Shirazad pauses in her narrative, and looks up to face the Sultan, and waits.

And the Sultan speaks.

'I have heard tales of dervishes who give away their money to the poor, as an example to those who would be blinded by riches. But I also know of treacherous servants and slaves. And I have heard tales of foolish kings who have been tricked into desiring things that could not be delivered.'

And so Shirazad continues, carefully.

'The king decides that he will have the treacherous carpenter flayed alive and then burnt to ashes. So he gives the order, and the vizier's men commence to put him to death.'

There is a long silence. The Sultan half closes his eyes, nods serenely, looking into the distance, beyond the moonlit courtyard.

'But that is not all…' Shirazad resumes. 'That night, restless in his bed of gold and amid curtains of purple, the king is having a disturbing dream. It is a most outlandish and unusual dream, which has the power to reveal the secrets of life and death. If it pleases his Majesty, may I continue this story of the king's dream on the morrow?'

And the Sultan graciously nods his assent.

~~~

'One night, Asahuerus, king of a hundred twenty and seven provinces from India to Ethiopia, has a terrible dream. He dreams that he has been flayed alive and then burnt to death. But the dream does not end with this dreadful demise. In his dream, he awakes to find himself transported up into the sky by angels like winged sphinxes. And the angels take him to a place beyond the sky, a place called Heaven. They tell him that this is where he will reside forever after.

'And the angels show him a beautiful land of eternal spring, with fertile valleys and glades, and snow-capped mountains, and watered by sparkling streams. At the centre of this land, there is a magnificent palace. He thinks he recognises the layout from somewhere...Yes, I can describe it.

'There is a great courtyard, at the centre of which is a splendid fountain in the form of four golden lions, each of whose mouths is a fountain, gushing out in the four directions of the compass, representing the four rivers of Paradise. One river is of milk, another of honey, a third of oil and a fourth of wine. Round the courtyard are four doors of gold. Behind the first door, there is a delightful garden, with a menagerie of tame animals and full of birds singing. Behind the second door, there is an orchard with many wonderful vines and fruits from lands all over the world. Behind the third door, there is a treasury of precious stones and jewels. And behind the fourth and final door, a storehouse of magic carpets, ebony horses, anatomical simulacra and other wonderful machines and conveyances.

'After looking at many such wondrous things, the angels then show the king the royal apartments of the palace, and there are walls of marble, pillars of ebony, and carpets of silk. There awaiting them is a magnificent throne of gold encrusted with pearls. And there are sofas with cushions covered with the finest silks and linens. In another room they see a table laid out for a great banquet, with plates of silver and vessels of gold. And as they pass the kitchens they smell a glorious aroma, and look in to see a great roast ox sizzling on a spit, and tables with sweetmeats and delicacies from far-off lands across the seas.

'All around the palace there are courtiers and eunuchs, servants and slaves going about their business, ready to serve every need and desire of their master.

'Then the angels take the king Asahuerus past the private royal apartments, where, they explain, no man other than the ruler may enter, except on pain of death. Then, behind sumptuous curtains, the king catches a glimpse of a beautiful young lady, reclining on a couch. And then the whole room opens up to reveal several more comely maidens, each more beautiful than the last, resplendent in silks and satin robes, with strings of pearls around their necks, and jewelled bracelets around their wrists and ankles. Besides these concubines, there are slave-girls—also beautiful—who are tending on their mistresses, combing their hair, or anointing their skin with fragrant oils. And the king asks if the ladies in the harem are virgins, and the angels assure him that they are all pure, and all the slave-girls, too. The king admits that he is impressed by the palace, and thinks that perhaps it is not so bad to die, if one can live an eternal life here.

'And so in his dream, in such a way, the king Asahuerus is shown all the rooms in the heavenly palace.

'Finally, the angels take him to see the dungeons. As they go down into the dark, they are struck by the stench of death, and the ghastly groans and pitiful cries of the still living. And they look down into three pits. In the first, they can just make out the broken figure of a man, whose body has been sorely scourged and singed and battered into a sombre silence. Then in the next pit they can see no-one in the darkness, but can hear someone gnawing at their own tongue. By the time they reach the third pit, they see and hear nothing, but can only smell burnt flesh.

'And the king asks who these wretched people are, or were. The angels tell Asahuerus that these were enemies of the state: rebels who had defied or disparaged or disobeyed the ruler of the palace. The angels assert that no righteous person should mourn their fate. Indeed, the righteous are permitted to watch the torment of the wicked. This is part of the reward of heaven—I am told.'

The Sultan nods gravely, and says: 'This heavenly palace certainly offers the prospect of a felicitous afterlife. But this paradise does not have anything that the Sultan does not already possess. The Sultan has all the finest foods and rarest wines. He can command the will of any man, upon pain of death. He can throw his enemies in dungeons, and have them tortured at his pleasure. The Sultan may ravish as many virgins as he pleases. (And if he should tire of ravishing virgins, he may venture incognito into the streets, if he wishes pleasures on different terms.) It seems as if this heavenly afterlife is no more than the continuation of a Sultan's life, but for all eternity.'

'You are perspicacious, as ever, Your Majesty,' says Shirazad, with downcast eyes; then looks up.

'But that is not the end of the story. The king Asahuerus is, you will recall, being shown the heavenly dungeons. After a while, he finds the dark and unpleasant smells and noises too tiresome and vexatious. His mind turns to more pleasant thoughts—of feasting on ox, or perhaps ravishing a slave-girl before supper. So he asks the angels when he might access his apartments, and start issuing commands.

'But the angels reply that this is out of the question. They tell him: "This palace is not yours to possess and enjoy. The royal apartments are not yours to live in. The throne is not yours, to rule from. The servants and eunuchs are not your chattels, to receive your command. The beautiful concubines are not yours to cherish; nor are the slave-girls yours to ravish. Rather, your place is this dungeon, here to languish, and hereafter be punished."

'And with that, he is thrown into the last of the pits.

'So Asahuerus, the erstwhile king of Shushan, finds himself in chains in the bottom of a pit, and whose only company is a charred carcase and an agitated scratching of rats. He weeps in despair over his wretched fate.

'Then, after three days and nights, just when he feels that he must expire, a door opens, and a hooded man arrives. He wonders if this is a jailer, or maybe torturer or executioner. And the king is very afraid, and prepares to face the worst.'

Shirazad pauses once more.

The Sultan nods and says: 'I suppose that the king is about to be cruelly put to death. But I appreciate that in addition to physical torture, the angels have first tormented him in his mind, by promising him things—a felicitous new life—that he cannot have.'

Shirazad resumes: 'It turns out that the hooded visitor is not an executioner, but has arrived from the world below. If it pleases your Majesty, I will tell the fate of the king and his mysterious visitor on the morrow.'

And the Sultan readily accedes to this request.

~~~

'In his dream, Asahuerus of Shushan, king of one hundred twenty and seven provinces from India to Ethiopia, is languishing in the prison of the heavenly palace, where he has been visited by a hooded man who could be a jailer, torturer or executioner. But the newcomer is none of these things: when he takes off his hood he reveals the flayed and scorched face of Didymus, the humble carpenter-slave. And Asahuerus, shocked, asks Didymus what they are doing here in this terrible place.

'And Didymus tells the king that he has incurred the wroth of the ruler of the palace. Then Asahuerus asks bitterly: who is this wretched ruler? And Didymus tells him that the palace is owned by the King of Heaven. This King of Heaven possesses all the riches one could imagine, and all the most beautiful things in the world. The King suffers people to live with him in heaven, but they live only to serve the King. Every inhabitant of heaven is either a servant or slave or eunuch. Their only pleasure is the King's pleasure. They are all owned by him; he may dispose of them as he wishes. Those who will not serve him on these terms are doomed to eternal torment as his prisoner.

'But, says Asahuerus, this sounds like the absurd and tragic rule of a cruel and self-indulgent King. Didymus replies that there are many cruel and self-indulgent kings whose reigns are absurd and tragic. Asahuerus looks up at the carpenter searchingly. And Didymus explains that it is Asahuerus' own cruelty that has brought him his fate in this dungeon. Aghast, the king asks if he might be spared.

'And Didymus says, yes, but the king needs to do two things. First, to be released from the dungeon, he must submit to all terms of the King of Heaven forever more. Asahuerus readily agrees. Secondly, says Didymus, if wishing to be granted a return to his former life, the king must look into his own heart, and be just and merciful to his subjects in the one hundred twenty and seven provinces from India to Ethiopia. And Asahuerus weeps, and gratefully promises that, if spared, he most certainly will.

'At that, the king wakes up to find that he had not, after all, died, but has just been dreaming. He finds himself back in his own earthly palace, in his bed of gold and amid curtains of purple. His vizier and attendants are clustered around him. He utters the name of Didymus, and asks about the fate of the carpenter. A servant is sent to the dungeons, and returns apprehensively with the news that, since his Majesty had ordered a slow death for him, the prisoner has yet to expire. Would His Majesty like to order a more immediate dispatch? The king, visibly shaking with relief, orders the prisoner to be released and brought directly to him.

'And so the flayed and scorched body of a man is dragged in, and flung at the king's feet. But the king in turn prostrates himself before the half-dead carpenter, and begs his forgiveness. He recounts his dream, and asks how it might be interpreted.

'Didymus slowly stirs, and haltingly tells the king that the things we do in this life build the foundations for what is to come in the next. And that he, Didymus, had been helping secure the king residence in the heavenly palace, and would continue to help him if he so desired. The king agrees and says that he will be just and generous in all his actions in future. He will not need any new earthly palace, but will continue to pay Didymus in gold and silver, to distribute to the needy as he sees fit. What's more, he shall strive to build a better life for himself in the eternal palace of the King of Heaven.

'And that, now, is the end of the story, Sire.'

The Sultan looks up and says to Shirazad: 'Yours is indeed a fine tale, that is not surpassed by any other fable of adventures in magical places. This idea of a heavenly afterlife is intriguing. However, it is unsatisfying; unedifying; and ultimately unacceptable. This Sultan should not wish to live like that wretched Asahuerus, as a eunuch in someone else's palace.'

A silence falls once more between storyteller and listener, and a tension can be sensed, as a gentle zephyr plays once more in the leaves of the almond trees.

'Your majesty. I have another ancient tale, from Mesopotamia. It tells of a man and woman, whose family and descendants were condemned to live every day waiting on death, and every night pleading to be spared by their Master.'

The Sultan looks directly into the eyes of Shirazad, and the candle flame flickers in his eyes. Her heart beats a little faster. Then he replies: 'The premise of this story indeed intrigues me, and it shall please me to hear it on the morrow.'

And so begins another tale of tales: the tragedy of Adam and Eve.

The Ghost-Writer from Hell

Deep beneath the streets and cellars of old Edinburgh, some say, there is another city lying beneath the city. Tales are told of scanty livelihoods scratched from underground vaults and cellars. Others lament desperate souls lost to vice and ruin in the basement bars and brothels. Yet darker yarns whisper of plague-infested streets sealed up and built over, entombing their wretched inhabitants alive. But the reality is deeper and darker than this…

Descent

The city is at its most sultry this time of year, and the overbearing sky not too bright, as I ready myself for my journey. I make light work of packing my leather case and the canvas knapsack that I carry on my back, filled with its tender cargo.

I make my way down a steep Old Town close, and disappear into an almost hidden doorway, which I open with an antique key. Once inside, I proceed downwards into darkness by a well-trodden staircase that serves as an ancient short-cut below.

I continue deeper and down countless more stairs and spirals, dark step after dark step, leather boot on grubby, smooth-worn stone. The going is not difficult, as my case is almost empty and my knapsack is well balanced on my back. I am, in any case, naturally sure-footed, despite my encumbrances, and I pause to take off my boots to gain a better grip, dark step after dark step, navigating curving pressing stone stairwells by dint of footstep and fingertip.

As I progress downwards, the temperature is getting palpably warmer. I find myself embraced by stale air that has become dank and heavy. As I plumb the bowels of the city they call Auld Reekie, my nostrils inhale assorted sour and pungent-smelling vapours that could overwhelm a wretched mortal who should stumble here.

At length, I sense the preternatural darkness opening out and a strange breathless emptiness before me, with only the blackness of an unseen undercroft for a sky, as if in some entombed region of the world that knows no stars. Then there is a barely perceptible gusting of wind, and then I made out a far-off sound, like a wail or a groan. In this cavernous space, the ground is now smooth and level; and below, I can just make out something at once incongruous and yet reassuringly familiar: a pair of railway tracks.

I stop short of the edge of the platform I find myself standing on, and lay down my canvas knapsack.

My eyes, naturally accustomed to the darkness, rest on the knapsack once more, and my mind drifts back up to the city of restless humanity above.

Tonight's haul is one of small bulk, but, as ever, high value. The transaction was one of the simpler, tragic cases, sprung by a pitifully small outlay of liquor: a token offer to purchase an unwanted burden; its acceptance precipitately called out as a crime, turning the would-be vendor into a desperate buyer of an illicit disposal, compounding the sin, which would secure us a hefty capital return of that unfortunate soul in good time, and the immediate dividend of their immoral issue in my custody—and, as a personal bonus, a minor act of depravity in my favour.

Presently there comes the sound of subterranean rumbling, and I make out a distant swaying light approaching, accompanied by scarlet sparks lightening up ghostly smoky plumes in the Stygian gloom. Then, there is an almighty shriek, and I behold a great steam engine now approaching, with a great blazing light, like the giant eye of a mechanical Cyclops, with its seething hissing pistons, and tumultuous puffing and wheezing, and hot metal clanking, hauling a stealthy train of carriages!

The train comes to a hissing, wheezing shuddering halt. A carriage door comes to rest directly before me—and I duly board.

Then, as the train lurches back into motion, with a great wheeshing and chuffing, I change out of my heavy outdoor clothes, then settle back in the naked comfort of darkness.

On Improvements in the Infernal Regions

The infernal regions have been subject to continuous improvement since antiquity—indeed since before the foundation of the World. It had long been recognised that the environs of Hell would need expansion and improvement to cope with the number of arrivals from its extensive hinterland. The infrastructure of the region is focused on the rust-red walled City of Dis; all iron roads lead sooner or later to this indefatigable Capital of Hell. Seat of the parliament of Pandemonium, the city has metal-clad walls with a vast moat, flaming red towers and eternal flues. Outside the City of Dis proper, the gaslights of the infernal suburbs stretch as far as the eye can see; and beyond them an inexorable permanent way of perdition now connects to all the tributary cities and lands above.

Over the course of history, Hell has been ceaselessly swollen by the influx from above, so that the population of this domain comfortably exceeds that of the whole World; the swarming multitudes of the chief metropolis of Hell make it easily the single most populous human settlement of all time.

The advent of steam power has greatly facilitated the operation of the place. The transport of coals, the movement of oils, fuels and excrement, and not least the movement of bodies, is aided by the use of railway tracks that have been especially built around these regions. Infernal steam engines clank around railway sidings and depots, their smoking chuffing and puffing resonating with the traditional fiery and smoky repertoire of this place. Here and there we see the billow of thick black smoke and cinders as some gallant steam engine goes about its infernal business, hauling dirt-encrusted wagons of bones and entrails.

The fires of hell are stoked continuously, aided by the prodigious mechanical apparatus of the modern age. Vast stockpiles of coal and shale are kept. The coal and shale are mined directly from seams under the Earth. Elsewhere, great spoil heaps of cinders and ash are piled up, forming a grimy topography of damnation.

Improvements have also been made to the distribution of all the fluids, where a series of dams and artificial channels has created a chain of lakes of fire and brimstone. Carefully hewn culverts and iron-clad channels direct the streams of boiling blood to where it is needed. Rivers of excrement, for long ingeniously piped from the latrines of the world, are now aided by mechanical pumping from banks of ceaselessly churning machines. Auxiliary ditches writhe with worms and maggots. Great vats of boiling pitch and brimstone are kept constantly bubbling, their acrid smell advertising their ever-present capacity for scouring or scorching; and baths of acid kept also conveniently for the stripping of skin from bone.

The latest installation is a mechanically automated plain of burning sand, afflicted by rains of fire from above. This is akin to a vast theatre set, with trapdoors and pulleys, with the deathly spray of fiery sparks created by apparatus adapted from iron-foundries. Meanwhile, an automated system of baskets and trapdoors ensures that there is a sufficient supply of excrement, fresh from loosened bowels, at the ready to be pressed into service.

The buildings of the city loom large with menacing functionality. Over here we see some dark workhouse—looking like something between a prison and an abattoir—with an ingenious array of machinery, powered by steam-driven cogs and belts, for the manufacture of all manner of iron implements for various probing and cleaving operations, and the chains and grappling-hooks to maintain a judicious degree of restraint. And over there we may observe a vast infernal hospital where broken bodies are treated to compulsory repairs.

Disembarkation

I awake with a lurch. All around me inky blackness, then a dim hint of a light. Our infernal train seems to have come to a stop. I hear footsteps, and a pair of eyes seems to look through me before moving on.

The incoming trains come to a halt here at a platform lit by flaming torches. Swarthy porters can be seen striding along the side of the train, roughly yanking open the doors of the carriages, to disgorge a wretched assembly of sweating, dishevelled looking people—by the looks of it, a general assortment of labourers, farm-hands, clerks and servant-classes; along with the occasional better-dressed person who might be a politician or clergyman. Some are in their working clothes, others in various states of undress.

Some of these travellers are clearly anguished and openly wailing. Others look bowed, even broken; sullen, wretched, as if already resigned to the fate that awaits them. Yet others are cursing and openly blaspheming, compounding their sins; or staggering in a drunken stupor, whether this being a cause or a consequence of their present predicament, I cannot say.

Then, further along, doors are opened to what appear to be the first-class carriages. Gingerly there emerge from the inside some bewildered looking passengers, moving slowly as if in a state of dazed disbelief.

I see one delicate lady swoon with fright as, alighting from her carriage to face a pack of surly wranglers, she realises the horrific reality of her situation. Too late, she regrets her teenage dormitory fornication and fondness for wearing mixed fibres. Her hat falls to the ground and is crushed underfoot. She has to be physically carried through the gates, grasped unceremoniously by an attendant, her limp defenceless female figure manhandled by rough ruddy forearms.

Another lady begs for mercy for her infant children, shaking her head piteously as if there has to be some mistake, for they are surely too young and innocent to meet such a fate. She sinks to her knees and looks beseechingly upwards, but can see no friendly sky, only the ceiling of their abyssal catacomb. The porter wrenches her to her feet and prods her forwards with her wailing charges.

The gentlemen are no less aghast. A mask of horror descends on one well-dressed gent, and he starts to mutter madly to himself. I see one poor fellow—nattily mustachioed and splendidly dressed, and looking for all the world like a 'devil-may-care' spirit, who has already evacuated his bowels into his fine linen breeches, and is now physically retching into a Stygian ditch.

A bespectacled professor is desperately brandishing a page of writing, as if demanding his rights, or pleading to be spared on some legal technicality about the classification of marine invertebrates. But it is all to no avail, as the attendant rips the page from his grasp. His otherwise pious but overimaginative wife is mortified to face the penalty for authoring blasphemous rumours about the King of Heaven's polygamous domestic arrangements. The troubled countenances of these unwary sinners turn to open horror as they realise—alas, too late!—their fateful destination.

On Improvements in the Infernal Regions (continued)

The economy of the infernal regions relies on the availability of raw materials and a plentiful supply of labour.

The mineralogical resources of the earth and rock are exploited by the ceaseless toil of a grimy workforce of sweating operatives. In some parts, they labour with agonising toil, working with picks and shovels to prise minerals from the reluctant earth. In other parts, where more urgent muscle is needed, armies of navvies and steam-shovel excavators are used for the job.

In the dark satanic mills a wretched workforce operates a multitude of looms ceaselessly, as they are worked to the bone. Every so often some unfortunate wretch is caught up and mangled in the machinery—like a steam-age rack of torture—but then expected presently to resume his Sisyphean labours. There are factories here, too, for making all the steam locomotives, railway tracks, iron cladding, and pipes and vats and trapdoors: all the infernal infrastructure of the modern age. Yet more poor souls do hard labour in the forges and factories that make the prods, irons, chains, bars, cleavers, cages and other instruments used in the more traditional industries of the place.

Nor are juveniles spared, but are put to use in the workhouse, making clothes, mechanical parts and other products needed in the infernal economy. Supple and dexterous youngsters are put to work cleaning the chimneys, flues and retorts of the blast furnaces. Meanwhile, down the deepest narrowest mineshafts, boys and girls alike toil in the heat, digging for coals and ores with their naked little hands.

As well as armies of manual labourers, there is also a phalanx of administrators carrying out the lettered work of the place: the keeping of records of the population, their various stations and employments, as well as ledgers of supplies, maps of mines and engineering works. They grapple with the ceaseless tide of paperwork not only by written records and accounts, but also using steam-powered printing presses and calculating-engines.[†]

The workforce is kept in bondage by the willfulness of its own making. The running of the place is ensured by a dedicated, well-drilled team of devils and demons, organised in an effective hierarchy of command. They go about their business with a certain rough efficiency. Their toil is ceaseless, keeping the great infernal Machine grinding onwards through the eternal Night.

Despatch

After handing over my own little bundle of joy, I watch

[†]Even the lot of the scribe is, dare one say, not easy. Here, the work is arduous and judiciously disagreeable after its own way; the workforce is cooped up in ranks of work-benches, with barely room to move, scribbling their pens and tapping on infernal typing machines, until their hands and wrists are weak and their eyesight worn and ruined. Writers do not have the satisfaction of self-expression, their narrative being composed on behalf, and at the behest, of superiors. Their only respite is in occasional external sorties as reconnoiterers or wranglers, to directly extract human resources or intelligence from the world above, in variously harsh, bright and cold working conditions.

from a discreet distance as the doomed passengers are groomed for final disposal. Their possessions are unceremoniously removed from them. Carefully packed bags and boxes are slung over into a large holding area. Umbrellas and walking-sticks are cast aside. Individual personal properties are wrenched from their erstwhile owners. A lady dressed in black clutches a delicately calibrated astronomical instrument, and a peculiar casket of russet-coloured rocks and dust, but these are torn from her and thrown into the pile with all the other detritus. A gentleman's collection of leather-bound manuscripts is tossed to the ground; a shrunken head escapes from an insufficiently secured satchel. I see one lady wrestle to keep hold of a daguerreotype image of her family; but it is soon torn from her, and dumped in a large pile with the other possessions, most of which will soon be incinerated.

Next, the new arrivals are relieved of all their money, yielding an assortment of cash, wallets, purses and portmanteaux. Then, they are required to surrender the remainder of their personal possessions, divulging a pathetic haul of now useless human trinkets: timetables and opera glasses, jewels and pearls, keys and combs, fountain pens and pocket watches, rosary beads and crucifixes.

Then I watch as, aghast and uncomprehending, the passengers are forced to strip: first overcoat and waistcoat and jacket, then belt and buckle and boot and shoe. With rising anxiety come shirt and blouse, trouser and stocking, and then garter and girdle and bustle, unto the last most reluctant undergarment: tossed aside in a hopeless heap of haberdashery and hosiery. And with those are cast off all the worldly pretensions of rank, affectations of taste and stamps of social distinction. Landowner and street urchin, professor and peasant, lady of the manor and pitiful daughter of the workhouse or whorehouse are now exposed as just so many trembling specimens of humanity: male and female they stand, young and old, dark and fair, tall and short, lean and stout.

Then a small gang of operatives advance with branding irons, knives, razors, pliers and saws. One by one the captives are prodded forward, trembling with fear, and then their bodies are held down and shorn and shaven all over. A crippled body has its wooden leg hacked off; a mouth cries out as its gold-capped teeth are yanked out with rough dexterity. The condemned are then pushed and prodded like beasts across the platform into the trucks of another train waiting. This time it is a goods train.

With a demonic shriek and blasts of smoke and sparks the human waste train pulls away, and the huddle of flesh and bone resumes its last journey as human cargo.

On Improvements in the Infernal Regions (concluded)

For all that there have been improvements in the physical machinations of Hell, the nature of evil has not changed. As night follows day, sinners succumb to temptation. A solemn diet of punishment awaits, so those who sinned in life face eternal torment in the afterlife.

An efficacious administration is necessary to ensure the fulfillment of Eternal Justice. As is written in scripture, anyone whose name is not found in the Book of Life shall be thrown into the Lake of Fire. The use of mechanical calculating engines and typewriters has, we believe, reduced the chance of eternal damnation through any administrative or typographical error.

The traditions of Hell are ancient, but the new mechanical means allow a greater variety of torments, and a much accelerated rate of dispensation of divine justice. The new sluices of scorching fire and brimstone are now better equipped to apply a continuous stream of torment—'forever and ever', as is written in scripture.

Likewise, the provision of apparatus for the scorching by fierce heat is purposefully accomplished, in fulfillment of the Good Book. Likewise, in the medical area, a laboratory dispenses efficacious administration of malignant sores. These fulfill the decreed will that the punished shall gnaw their own tongues because of the pain. For each sin has its place: observe here, those who succumb to fornication, or sell their body for sin; there, witness those who dispose of their own ill-begotten offspring, tormented in turn by their diminutive victims. And let us not forget the infernal nurseries for unbaptised infants, equipped with banks of miniature ovens and incinerators for the roasting and curing of original sinners.

Everything here is running its retributive course as it should, in fulfillment of the grand Plan. Demons and devils unremittingly deliver the will of their superiors, obeying orders in a great chain of command, all the way up to the one ultimate Authority.

All over the infernal region, in workhouse, pit or hospital, all is prison, all is torture chamber, all is charnel-house.

All is done as it is written.

And as I look out over My Creation, I see that it is Good.

Meeting the Gods-in-Law

It's all nicely casual and cosy—just me, God, His mother, and of course His Father, God, Senior. I'm still a little nervous, though. After all, it's the first time I am meeting my long-term partner's parents—the prospective Gods-in-law.

We arrive in good time at God's parents' lovely old townhouse in a leafy enclave of south Jerusalem overlooking Beit Lehem Street and the Old City. Our introductions are a little self-conscious. How do you correctly address the Mother of God? Or God the Father, face to face, when the Son is in the same room? ('Just call Me Father.') I compliment the Gods on the beautiful flowers and vines in their garden, and we soon settle down to a lovely evening on their roof terrace.

God Senior has an instant sense of presence, with His gaunt face with shining eyes, but He's shorter than I imagined; He is conservatively dressed, with the look of a time-served ex-military character who could still be handy in a fight. God's mum is younger than I imagined, albeit with silvery hair, thin wire-rimmed spectacles, and plainly dressed but with a flash of colour. She turns out to be quite the hostess, with a wonderful supper of spicy carrot soup, smoked tuna, shakshuka and home-made bread. God supplied the wine, on our behalf. I've also brought some fresh figs from our own little garden. God's mum smiles and seems to appreciate the gesture.

Soon enough, my prospective in-laws are asking me the usual questions—about my family, my parents' busi-ness, and my relationship with God. Our conversation sails along the surface swimmingly, though it doesn't take long for things to turn personal. At one point God's mum asks straight out if I'm pregnant—although I sus-pect she's really more interested in if I am a virgin.

(I say, not as far as I know.)

The elder God causes a wind to blow on the surface of His soup and says, 'As long as she knows what she's letting herself in for.'

'I'm sure she'll be fine,' says Mrs God. 'I'm sure God will make sure of that.'

I'm still not sure of the history between God's par-ents, which always seemed a bit of a mystery, even to God. But as a family they seemed like your typical feisty middle-class Jerusalem household. It seems that they were always arguing over politics, religion, music, litera-ture…Between them, God and His parents and siblings held all shades of opinion from a kibbutz-inspired sec-ular communism to fundamentalist Zionism.

They quarrel over the Middle East, like everything else. God Senior is all for more direct military intervention by the Western democracies (the hawks were right about that). He sees the Iraq war as a righteous cause; a textbook case of a just war. And it isn't long before that particular heat-seeking conversation is headed our way.

'Wouldn't *you* take up arms against tyrants or terrorists? Being a peacenik is all very well—in times of peace—but sometimes you have to fight. For your way of life, your people, your very existence. Sometimes the wicked need to be smitten, even if it means shedding blood of the innocent.'

God's mother would have preferred a multi-lateral solution, involving the United Nations, but when push came to shove, she stood by her man.

But God always reckoned there must be another way.

'All those innocent civilians, all those children blown to pieces…for what? Just for the abstract ideal of democracy, to show the world who's boss?'

The elder God lobs a small tomato into His mouth and a testing question in my direction. 'So, what do you think of the situation in Judea and Samaria? Do you think, like this guy, you don't need to be pro-Israel just because you're Jewish?'

I was used to treading carefully through the minefield of Israel-Palestine relations, but arguing with someone with a personal territorial stake was always going to be tricky.

'Well I think you can be pro-Israel without meaning you need to support every Israeli government policy…

Otherwise, well, there could be no opposition in Israeli politics…and so no democracy. Then where would we be?'

God's mother smiles as if appreciating my carefully weighted answer. But God is busy preparing his own counter-offensive.

'Father would be all for a bit of good old-fashioned theocratic despotism,' He sneers, tearing his bread theatrically.

But the elder God is undaunted.

'Look, Son, Thou canst not just "turn the other cheek", so to speak, when Thou art the Commander-in-Chief.'

'But the meek…'

'The meek can only inherit the Earth—or anything—if the strong take the moral high ground and enforce the laws of the land.'

God plays with His shakshuka sulkily. Perhaps His Father has a point.

'Look Son, this land is Ours by right, and don't Thee forget it. It's all very well doing outreach in Afula or civil defence in Rishon LeZiyyon, but sometimes you have to come and fight on the front line.'

They glare at each other, before resuming Their food.

God has a big thing about human rights, for refugees and indigenous peoples around the world. It's one reason He is reluctant to follow His Father's footsteps.

And He would never want to see anyone oppressing or conquering peoples and territories in His name. ('Take Me outside and shoot Me, if I ever let that happen…')

God Senior has made light work of His fish, carefully arranging the bones around the side of the plate, seemingly savouring the handiwork on each one.

'Remember, the World does not owe Thee a living.'

It seems to be a bone of contention that God shows no inclination to follow His family's traditional calling. One of God's brothers is a kabbalist rabbi in Sefad, while a sister has become some sort of hippy internet guru somewhere in California. But God's calling is to be an itinerant grassroots activist, fighting for human rights, irrespective of ethnicity. He's campaigned in Hebron, and even visited Arab villages in the West Bank ('it's My land too'). But His Father doesn't see that as a proper job, or a fitting living for one from His own Loins.

'I mean, how wilt Thee be able to support a family? Thou wouldst need to get Thyself a proper job then, wouldstn't Thou?'

'Father, cut Me some slack, please. Thou know I have to find My own way.'

It's clear that there is a generation gap between Father and Son. I could see straight away that a lot of the time, they just don't see eye to eye. But then, I could also see that they were in some ways so alike: God is, after all, His Father's Son. They were both men of conviction; both sure they were right, and unwilling to give an inch on anything. But when it came to values, there was a clear divergence.

God Senior takes the Torah as the absolute authority, to be observed faithfully like His forefathers. My God saw doing the right thing in your heart as more important than observing all the old laws. And, while the elder God was ultimately happy to settle down, with a nice house, my God challenged Him by saying we should give our riches away (though I will keep my own bank account). The Father would get mad and accuse His Son of being an idealist, a liberal, a socialist.

I could also see that God was exasperated that His Father, though obviously fallible, was so self-satisfied, pretty much set in His ways, as if He had already worked everything out, as if He were above the fray, as if He'd never had any struggles of His own. Whereas my God at least could acknowledge temptation and doubt and fear, and judge people only after having been in the shit Himself. But then, I suppose I am privileged that He opens up to me, shows His vulnerable side. I can't really judge any other God.

But most fundamentally, the elder God, despite his appeals of tolerance, was really an old-school social conservative, and didn't approve of how His Son lived His life.

'You and Your city crowd, with their fancy cosmopolitan ways. Hanging out with all those…lushes and low-lifes, beach bums and wiener-eating libertines, oh yes, oh so fashionably amoral. In the old days We'd call them Godless sinners, heathens and harlots!'

'It's just as well I never bring My friends back here then, Father' says God. 'Thou wouldst be an embarrassment.'

'Well, not if they're Thy Tel Aviv toyboys…'

'They're not…'

'…ladyboys; whatever.'

'I don't know why Thou art so harsh on them, Father. They are not harming anyone else.'

'I think Thou wilt find that they are sinning in the eyes of the LORD!'

'Wouldst Thou not forgive Thine own Son?' says Mrs God, gently.

A divine eyebrow inclines, then falls into a frown again.

'Self-abuse is one thing. Crushed *cojones* are another. But no Sodomite is welcome in My house.'

After a silence, He looks up as if to say, What have I said?

'A sin is still a sin, even if it is forgiven.'

A moody pause ensues, and morsels of food studiously pursued.

'Er, would Anyone like any coffee?' says God's mother.

Father and Son grunt approval in unison. God mops us the last of His shakshuka with a bit of bread, while God Senior takes a large swig to finish His wine. He gestures at the empty bottle; God shrugs but stays put.

I help God's mum take the dishes to the kitchen.

'I hope you don't get the wrong impression,' she says. 'Father's a good person. He means well. But He is very single-minded, and can seem dauntingly righteous sometimes, and that *can* be hard to live with. He loves His Son dearly, of course, but it's sometimes hard for God to love Him back.'

'That's okay, I understand,' I say, looking around for the bin to put the fish bones in. 'Though I guess it must be tough for you, keeping Them both happy?'

'Yes, being both the mistress of God, and the mother of God…'—she has a wry laugh. 'You know, ever the wife in the kitchen and the virgin in the bedroom! It's an impossible job sometimes, and you don't always get the thanks. But I've no regrets.'

I could see there was more to being God's girlfriend than I'd thought.

'But *you* need to be sure what you're letting yourself in for.'

'It's okay, I'm going in with my eyes open. God's been very good.'

'Yes, I can see that.' She sighs. 'But you know, that's no less than His Father before Him. He was always good to me. I mean, I was so young, innocent…He could have had anyone He wanted; but He chose me.'

Not for the first time, I struggle to imagine the possibly messy or embarrassing circumstances of their courtship and consummation.

'You know, He defied His own Father to go with the likes of me…So you see, your God may think He's so radical; but He's not the first Son to rebel, or do things differently from His Father.'

I must admit, I find it hard to imagine the elder God as a reckless or rebellious youth, sowing His wild oats out in the sticks. But it's a line I pursue when I return to the table.

'So, let me get this right, er, Father. You were a wild one, too, in your, er, Thy youth?'

I think I see Him suppress a smile, as He scratches His beard. 'Oh yes, of course! I could be the life and soul of the party, like anyone else. In My day, I was a bit of a trailblazer Myself—defied My own Father too.'

God sighs and rolls His eyes, looking as if He's heard it all before, and makes a show of exiting to the bathroom.

But God Senior warms to the theme.

'You may think I'm a tough old bastard, but you should have seen *My* Father. You should have heard the arguments in Our household. My Own Father used to rant and rage and say He had a good mind to throw Me out the house. To wish I had never been born.'

God's mother brings the round of coffees, with baklava and a few of our figs.

'God's a liberal compared to those Who came before Him!' says Mrs God, caressing Her Husband's shoulders. 'You should have seen *His* Father—your God's grand-God.'

'Now He had had a tough life, right enough. He had been in the wars, actually seen action. Life was cheap then. Death was just part of the job. Sometimes it was a matter of instant obedience or instant death. Some of His children were so scared of Him, He reduced Them to trembling wrecks. It wouldn't be allowed nowadays. And He said *His* Father would have *killed* Him, for sure, if He had defied Him like I did. So don't let God make Me out as the Bad Guy.'

God returns with a fresh bottle of wine, and some old family albums. These are a real eye-opener.

'Now there's My dear old Father,' says the elder God, bringing out his bifocals for a better look. He's pointing to a blurry image of some ancestral God in the wilderness, Who belched smoke like a volcano.

'Was He the one with the hairy legs?'

'No, that was an earlier God—Who walked in the Garden. No, this Guy was carried around in a tent.'

I am finding it a little difficult to follow all the Gods. Some Gods have more than one name; some names apply to different Gods. They all have Their own personalities and peccadillos, though you could tell some of the traits were carried down the generations.

'Your grand-God railed against all forms of sexual transgression,' explains the elder God. 'If You think I'm bad, You should have seen Him. Oh, He was obsessed with sex—He raged against every sort of carnal sin.'

'The only thing We knew about His own sexuality was that He must have managed it at least once,' says Mrs God mischievously.

'But then take the God of Babel—He was more of a libertine,' says God, eyeing His Father.

'Don't you also have relatives in Mesopotamia?' I ask.

'Oh, We don't talk about Them,' says God.

'We lost track of the Mesopotamian Gods,' says the elder God. 'That line probably died out ages ago.'

'Or inter-married,' says God's mother lightly.

'So, how far back have You managed to trace Your relatives?' I say.

'Oh, right back—to before there were any Hebrew Gods at all.'

'Take My great-great-grand God,' says God. 'He was a bad-tempered old bastard if there ever was one. You fell out with Him, You fell out forever.'

'But before Him was an even older one—as far as we can tell, the original God. Now He was a rum one. Not only was He relaxed about sex, but positively encouraged it. In fact, it was His primary recommendation!'

'We don't know much else about Him. Except that, as Our oldest ancestor by definition, obviously, He must have existed. Or else We wouldn't be here, would We?'

'It's amazing that You can follow Your family line of Gods continuously down thousands of years,' I muse.

'True,' says God. 'But at the same time, They were all so different in Their Own ways. Take Our earliest ancestors. They mostly kept Themselves to Themselves. They didn't express any humanity or love in those days. But then, They didn't demand worship or sacrifice, either.'

'They spent more time talking to people—though maybe less time listening,' says God's mum.

'And things can change again,' says God, warming to his theme. 'Believe Me, when I become Father, I will do things My way. I will be just like I am now. I will be a different kind of Father, You'll see. You won't catch Me strutting around, demanding sacrifice or hero-worship from My Children.'

'Look, Son, it's all very well having Your liberal ideas now. Thy private life is up to Thee. Thou canst let Thyself go—get Thy End away—even defy My name. But once Thou becomes a Father Thyself, Thou hast to settle down and behave. As Father, Thou art the ultimate moral authority. So Thou wilt need to sort out Thy values. I mean, Son, some of Thy morals are so liberal, they are hardly morals at all. Sometimes, I think, Thou mayest as well be some wishy-washy multi-cultural secularist.'

I look sideways at God. We have, in fact, been considering our own values, and which we'd like to pass on if we have a family of our own. The liberal, inclusive path seems not such a bad way to go.

'Well, would that really matter, if there is a patter of little Gods around the Garden, as long as they are happy?' says God's mum, looking at God and me.

And it dawns on me that the down-to-earth human values, which I appreciate most about God, must come mostly from His mother's side.

'Wishy-washy!' says God. 'I don't think so. Half the people think I've gone all secular. Another half think I'm the Messiah—or an agent of Beëlzebub. And the rest think I've sold out, inventing a new religion. I can't be all of those!'

They nod sympathetically.

'Look, just because I rebel, doesn't mean I'm any less Your Son. Just because I promote human values, doesn't mean I can't be a God. And just because I'm a liberal or radical doesn't mean I'm any less Jewish. Nothing's going to change that, as long as I live.'

As we sip our coffees, I reflect that the evening has gone really well. God's Family aren't as crazy or daunting as I had feared. God's mum is fantastic; she has made me feel so welcome, and, well, normal. And meeting God's Father, well He's not as bad as God had warned. Indeed talk of all His ancestors has helped to put God in His proper perspective.

But at the end of the day, God is His Own man.

And that will do just fine for Me.

Jerusalem, Midlothian

The Cowgate is not the most salubrious place for Jesus to find himself on a Saturday night out in Edinburgh. On the face of things, it's where you're most likely to find a rabble, a commotion, youths prowling around, people being chucked out of drinking dens. They say all human life is here: well-oiled lawyers and delinquent bankers cheek by jowl with brain-fried ravers and crack-headed beggars. Despite this—or perhaps because of it—Jesus can't help being drawn to this boisterous melting pot of a street.

Tonight, he's taking a zig-zag short-cut across the city, from Salisbury Crags to his garret behind the Grass-market. But now there's a commotion ahead, down one of the more squalid closes. There is some sort of a scuf-fle, a female yelp and a slap and a muffled squeal and the sound of a struggle. A couple of guys are manhandling a woman with torn clothes, yanking her along, dragging her off to a dark place.

Jesus can hardly just walk on by.

He thinks of the most passive-aggressive thing he can do: so he just stops dead, and faces them. They turn around, twisted faces, menace in their eyes. They have their prey, they must reckon they've earned it.

'Dirty filthy *hoor*,' says one of the thugs, as if by explanation.

Jesus stands his ground; has to think instinctively.

'Guys! Take me instead,' he says.

The thugs pause, as if not sure what to make of his unorthodox offer. By making himself vulnerable, Jesus has shown his own strength.

The pair just stand there, scowling and spitting. Jesus faces them down, like a Master showing his dogs who's boss. Then they throw the girl down into the dirt, and slope off into the night.

Jesus tries to check if the girl is all right, but she hurries off swiftly. He wonders if she really is a sex worker. He's known a few in his time; all good experience.

~~~

That the incarnate God once trod the streets and wynds of ancient Edinburgh is an extraordinary proposition, wrought from the bold imagination and brilliant iconoclasm of that indefatigable cosmic chronicler, William Comyns Beaumont.

The full story of cometary cataclysm and the role of Britain as crucible of world history is well told elsewhere, by Comyns Beaumont himself, and so I shall not rehearse that writer's narrative except in terms of its most singular revelation: that the Holy Land associated with the life and death of Jesus Christ was not, as had long been supposed, in Judea; but in Midlothian, Scotland; and that the biblical Jerusalem was actually located in the site of the present-day city of Edinburgh.

Comyns Beaumont's argument, in essence, is that the topography of the Bible better fits modern-day Edinburgh than the Levantine city now known as Jerusalem. According to Comyns, the biblical Citadel, or city of Zion, corresponds with Edinburgh Castle Rock; the Temple Mount is roughly where St Giles Cathedral now stands. The Pool of Siloam was the South Loch; the Pool of Bethesda was the Nor' Loch. The Dung Gate was King's Stables Gate, and the Water Gate was—fittingly enough—the Water Gate. Holyrood Palace was the Palace of the Cedars; the Mount of Olives, south-east of the city proper, is what we now know as Arthur's Seat.

Further afield, the biblical port of Joppa (Jaffa) corresponds with the small port of Joppa on the Firth of Forth. Tophet can be identified as Corstorphine Hill; this once fearful place of sacrifice is today found in the middle of a golf course (as Comyns Beaumont notes, matter-of-factly). The redoubtable eminence of Gogar Mount (Golgotha) is the solemn elevation where Christ was crucified.

According to Comyns Beaumont, it was an insurrection of the rebellious Jerusalem populace that led the occupying Romans to destroy the Caledonian city, from whose ruins the fort of Dun Eidinn would later emerge; while the Hebrew tribes were expelled and scattered to various parts of the world, including the Levantine territories of modern-day Israel and Palestine. It was to that latter location that Constantine the Great, the opportunistically Christian Roman Emperor, for his own political reasons had the biblical narrative relocated to the citadel of Jebus—renaming their new Jerusalem and its local landmarks after their counterparts in the ancient Caledonian burg previously known by that name.

Comyns Beaumont's message is of more than historical interest; it has a cosmic geological dimension of future portent. It is well known that James Hutton, the city's most celebrated geologist, once averred that the local rocks showed 'no vestige of a beginning, nor prospect of an end'. But the implications of Comyns Beaumont's thesis are that Caledonia must be one of the contenders for the place of creation where Man first trod the Earth, while the valley of Jehoshaphat—now reckoned to lie between Dumbiedykes and Salisbury Crags—is where the dead shall rise and the world shall end.

~~~

Jesus is in his favourite Canongate tavern sitting quietly in a corner, making some notes on a bit of paper, underlining here or scoring out there. A bunch of his mates arrive and join him. Jesus looks up and puts his notes away as they greet him.

'Man, what are you like? Aw your scribblings an' sayings!'

'Making up yer ain bible, eh?'

'Gie's peace, youse lot,' says Jesus. 'Ah'm still jist working it aw oot for masel'.'

'Aye, ever the rebel, eh?'

'Naw, Ah'm urnae,' says Jesus. 'Dinnae be thinkin' Ah've come tae destroy the law, or the prophets. Ah've come tae *fulfil* them.'

'Aye but you've really got up the authorities' noses. They rabbis'll surely no' let ye add aw they new stories intae the bible.'

'Look, Andy, you may think figuring out scripture is a waste ay time. And you may no' agree wi' aw ma interpretations. But at the very least Ah'm just drawing attention tae what the Buik actually says, ken?'

The friends nod in agreement.

'Ah mean, who of youse lot honestly ken what scripture really says, or really means? Aye right enough, you're told this, you're told that. About God, yon patriarchs, prophets… the laws, the chronicles… the history o' this city; you name it. But so many o' they self-righteous people who huv a go at me huv no' actually read what's writ in the bible. How can we get anywhere if even those who preach dinnae ken what the Guid Buik actually says? Or if they dae ken, they're no' telling *us*.'

'But does it matter, likesay?'

'Aye, why no' just live yer life, like the rest ay us?'

'Look, people round here are just gaun through the motions ae religion. Aye, they go tae the Temple right enough, and mibbe make a wee sacrifice, but they're more interested in looking efter their ain erses, than serving God, or helping ithers.

'If ye ask me, people are too quick to condemn, an' too slow to forgive. Ah mean, look at yon chancer over there—he's been sniffin' aroon yon wee bar lassie aw evening, and you'd bet he'd be up for a shag wi' her, right enough. But if he caught her in the act wi' someone else, he'd be happy to see her stoned for fornication.

'And they high heid yins are no better. A bunch ay hypocrites if ye ask me. *Say* one thing, *dae* anither. Then they take it out on me. I mean, so what if Ah huv a bevvy, hang out wi' aw sorts ay radge bastards, 'n huv a lassie as a bidie-in?'

'But isn't that gaun against God's laws?'

'As long as Ah serve ma God, and love ma neighbour, that's *aw* that matters!'

They look thoughtful; some still look doubtful.

'Jesus, man, Ah'll give ye this, ye're honest, and brave, to question they rabbis. But how do ye ken thit you are right?'

'Ah just know it, Tam; Ah feel it in ma bones,' says Jesus. 'Ah feel the Chief's telling me this is ma mission in life, likesay, whit Ah wis put on Earth for, ken?'

'But why you? Why here, why now?'

'Well, why no'?'

~~~

The reception of Comyns Beaumont's treatise was as electrifying as it was irresistible. Jerusalem became the instant talk of the town. Hardly could there be an Edinburgh public house or private home that did not ring with opinion on Comyns' astonishing hypothesis. For who would not be thrilled to envision the Son of God Himself pacing restlessly up and down Leith Walk, or flitting through the closes of the Old Town on His way to the market or Temple!

The newspapers had a field day reconstructing Jesus' back story and speculating about his personal life. Where did He hang out? Did He have a girlfriend? And was He a Catholic or a Protestant?

Schoolmistresses took their flocks on field trips to Calvary by the Union Canal. Students re-enacted the stations of the cross in pub crawls from the Grassmarket to the city boundary. Guided walks and ghost tours sprang up around the Old Town, revisiting the haunts of the Son of God.

But the city authorities were in a quandary. Some councillors felt that Comyns' Edinburgh could be a great boost for tourism, helping make the city an all-year-round destination. But others were nervous about the End of the World taking place so close to the city centre, and wondered if it could be a public order risk. Could it not be located somewhere else, like Glasgow?

While the universal Church of Rome gave a calculated ecclesiastical shrug to the question of the whereabouts of Jerusalem, the Church of Scotland was discombobulated by such a major geographical controversy on their doorstep. The conservatives were cautious of upsetting orthodoxy, while the radicals were ready to reignite an older tradition. After all, the Kirk's very existence was born of the self-confidence of Scotland being represented directly to the Almighty, without need of any intermediary authority. Why indeed should Edinburgh not be the City of God?

Academic geographers redoubled their attention to the sacred topography and toponymy of the city. Doctoral scholars traced the route where the bullock of sacrifice was led to the altar, and where Zedekiah escaped from Nebuchadnezzar. Archaeologists dug deep to expose the very paving stones that the feet of Jesus would have trod.

Historians speculated that Pontius Pilate was born in Perthshire; and that Constantine himself must have visited Caledonian Jerusalem while on military duty. A literary scholar recalled that the Devil had already appeared in Scottish history, recorded making a deadly summons in broad daylight in the centre of Edinburgh. Persistent rumours suggested that beneath the wynds of the Old Town there was a trapdoor to the nether world, used as a short-cut by agents of Satan to carry off sinful souls to Hell.

Wishful believers claimed that Jesus founded Rosslyn Chapel, and visited Glastonbury, even then a place of popular pilgrimage. A senior cleric averred that a personal acquaintance of his had once wrestled with an angel in a Glasgow bar.

And Comyns' account gained a flurry of speculative sequels. A lay preacher argued that Jesus actually hailed from Cowdenbeath in Fife, identifying Loch Leven as the Sea of Galilee, and the Hill of Beath as Gibeath-haa-raloth, or Hill of the Foreskins. A popular archaeologist claimed to have located the Garden of Eden near Kilmartin; a radical rival was convinced the Rivers of Babylon once flowed through Renfrewshire.

Comyns Beaumont's tract had undeniably stirred a renewed sense of spirituality and the immanence of divine reality; it is hard to imagine how things could have been otherwise. Comyns Beaumont societies sprang up around the country, and around the world. The city of Edinburgh, aroused from her slumber, was now ready to assume—or resume?—her proper place in the cosmos.

~~~

One day, up on Calton Hill, the children of God come before the Lord, and Satan also comes among them. The Lord says to Satan, 'Where'uv you been?' And Satan answers the Lord, saying, 'Fae going to and fro in the earth, and fae walkin' up an doon in it.' Both God and Satan know this city well: from the crags and cobbled wynds to wind-blown prospects, from ancient days to recent times. And God says 'Ah huv a job for you…'

Jesus' mission takes him to different parts of the city, meeting all sorts of people from all walks of life. He often goes for walks to the Mount of Olives on summer evenings. He always feels this uncanny sense of destiny as he treads through the Valley of Jehoshaphat, near Salisbury Crags, where bones will rise and the dead will come alive, before God shall sit in Judgement at the End of the World.

In his bedsit sometimes he stays awake all hours, and looks at the stars; and thinks of his future.

And the Lord God hovers over the city, with dark moods of weather.

Now one day, Jesus is fasting, out in the wilderness of West Lothian, on the parched plains after the road runs out beyond the Breich Water.

And a wind-blown Satan comes up, and says, 'Are ye no hungry?'

'Mibbes aye, mibbes naw,' says Jesus.

'So why no' turn aw they stanes intae loafs o' breid?'

But Jesus says, 'It's written in the Buik, "Man canna live on breid alane".'

Next time Satan's in town, he takes Jesus up to the parapets of the Citadel. They look out over the city, and Satan says, 'What's the point of life, eh?' And he looks down the rock face and says, 'So why no' just throw yersel' aff?'

And Jesus laughs and says, 'Naw, man, Ah dinnae think so.'

'How no, but?' says Satan. And he takes out a copy of a bible he has brought with him, and says, 'After all, it's written, "If ye trip up, ye'll be caught by angels", quoting from a psalm.

Jesus frowns and takes the bible from Satan and leafs through it a bit, then says, 'Mibbes aye; but, the Buik also says… "It's better no' tae try an' test God like that".

Then Satan shows Jesus all the lands and kingdoms as far as the eye can see, and says 'Aw this Ah'll gie ye, if ye'll gae doun on yir knees an wurship me.'

And Jesus looks out across the Firth of Forth, and says, 'Aw they lands, and the Kingdom of Fife an' aw?'

And Satan says, 'Aye, the Kingdom of Fife an' aw.'

Jesus makes a wry smile, and says, 'Naw, God's already promised me as much. On similar terms.'

Satan shrugs, and they part; they have both done what they had to do.

~~~

The conscientious reader may have already started to doubt the very idea that the incarnate God could come to be traipsing around the streets of urban Caledonia, rather than Judea. What hubris, to claim that Edinburgh should once have been the biblical Jerusalem, the city of God on Earth! That the Heart of Midlothian should be the figurative Navel of the Universe! Or that Christ

Himself should choose a modestly hilly spot off the A8 as the setting for His supreme sacrifice! Indeed, why should the LORD GOD, Almighty Creator of the World and Universe, alight on this particular craggy escarpment for His chosen people?

What we will never know is the extent to which Comyns Beaumont saw himself as a prophet, or even believed his own remarkable creation. Can he really have supposed that those feet of Christ trod those Caledonian cobbles? Or could Comyns himself have been seduced by the Devil in those dark bars and wynds of the Old Town?

Very little is known of the author's inner life. Despite availability of a published autobiography, one struggles to read the man between the lines. Certainly, in *Rebel in Fleet Street*, one looks in vain for a trace of the authentic voice of Comyns the prophet; no hint of historical Nephilim or geographical Phlegethon is to be found therein.

But then, while it may seem natural to question Comyns Beaumont's sources and motives, it seems never to occur to anyone to test the sources and motives of any other biographers of Jesus. After all, the improbable prospect that a bohemian Jesus and his burgeoning entourage were once Edinburghers requires less of a leap of faith than the miraculous conception, incarnation and resurrection of an as yet hypothetical, supernatural, anthropomorphic Deity.

Each of us must weigh up the relative likelihood of the story's concoction by a London journalist, of having Constantine's agents scrambling over arid plateaus of Judea, surveying topographical features and renaming them after their Midlothian counterparts—and then rolling out a gargantuan Roman propaganda machine to sustain the fabrication, for twenty centuries.

The sceptic might conclude that the whole affair is more likely to reveal something about the psyche of the narrator, or the human condition more generally: the burning need to believe there is some larger order to the cosmos, for each of us to be part of something bigger, and the longing for important things to happen among people like us, in places familiar to us—whether Gogar or Golgotha.

Ultimately, the idea that the axis of the world might pass through a small city on a rocky outcrop between the Pentland Hills and the Firth of Forth, rather than one between the Mediterranean and Dead Sea, need not be considered so far-fetched, in the cosmic perspective.

We might not be so surprised to learn that while Jesus of Nazareth lived out his mortal days in Judea, some ancient Pictish tribe knew that an indigenous God created the World near here, living in the holy lands of Midlothian with his divine offspring, who trod the Earth amidst crag and escarpment between the Pentlands and the Forth. Perhaps indeed old gods still haunt these parts; while their mortal sons and daughters yet tread the streets and wynds of Edinburgh, still seeking meaning in it all, and waiting for the end of the world.

The Gods' Extended Mess

High above the clouds, with the sun on my right and flying on through the stars, on the third day I arrived at heaven.

I found a door to the place, and knocked on it.

Presently, the door opened and the god Hermes appeared. He looked quite surprised to see a human mortal arriving at his door—not half as surprised as I was to find a heavenly door answered by a god dressed as a man.

He asked me to wait while he fetched Zeus. The lord of all gods soon arrived and cast a wary eye over me and asked, 'What is your name, and where are you from?'

'I am Lucian, of Samosata,' I replied.

'But how did you get here?' said Hermes.

So I told them how, inspired by Daedalus, I had fashioned a means of flight from wing of eagle and vulture, and ascended into the skies, leaving the Earth far below.

'And what do you want here?' said Zeus suspiciously.

'I am an adventurer and reporter, come to find out for myself the true nature of the gods, and of the heavens, and how those relate to us mortals on Earth.'

Also I hoped for a look around the place, and maybe get some dinner.

'Very well, I suppose you may visit us—but for no more than a day and a night,' said Zeus. 'It should do no harm if the people are reminded of our works from time to time.'

'Thank you, I shall be honoured to learn,' said I.

'As it happens,' said Zeus, 'I am about to go on duty, so you can see how things work around here. Please follow me.'

And so we went off to the part of heaven that was the best place for listening to prayers and receiving sacrifices. On the way, Zeus questioned me about matters on Earth: first the usual topics about the current price of wheat in Greece, and the latest fashions, and which of the gods were most popular among the mortals these days.

Presently we came to a place where there was a series of devices like holes with lids in them. Zeus explained that this was where the gods receive prayers and sacrifices from mortals. He admitted that he sometimes found it tiresome to deal with all the prayers sent up, and wished not to be bothered so much by the petty affairs of men. At least, though, it was not compulsory that gods should act on the prayers of mortals.

Zeus then suggested we go to receive some sacrifices. These were a customary means of nourishment and gratification for the gods. He sighed with satisfaction as he sniffed the aroma of some nice flame-grilled lamb from a pious shepherd from Anatolia.

Then Zeus issued some instructions to the winds and the seasons.

'It all seems to work wonderfully,' I suggested. 'Now I see it from up here, being a god does not seem too onerous.'

Zeus scowled. I added, as gravely as I could, 'Although it must be an awesome responsibility.'

'You are indeed perspicacious,' he said. 'A right-minded and resourceful person like yourself might be able to handle some divine duties while you are here. Perhaps you might like to try? Under Hermes' supervision, mind. I have a speech to attend to before dinner.'

And so it was that I almost accidentally became a god for a day. Actually, it was trickier than I had first thought, and I was not entirely clear that I had mastered the control of things, and I made a few errors early on. At first I reversed the north wind by mistake so that it came from the south, causing a lot of confusion in the Adriatic. I left a dry wind running for too long and nearly caused a drought in Thrace. But after a bit of practice, I seemed to get better at it, and delivered a good amount of rain in Scythia, applied some lightning in Libya, and about a thousand bushels of hail gently scattered over Cappadocia.

Hermes explained that as well as individual acts of the weather, they also had an ongoing committee attending to the long-term changing of the climate, which helped to determine whether the Earth should get warmer or cooler. Apparently the gods were always changing their minds, and arguing over whether the climate should go one way or the other, and whether in fact it was actually getting warmer or cooler, and whether it should be the committee's responsibility in the first place.

Then Hermes took me to another part of heaven, and allowed me to try some acts of creation. I managed to craft some small islands, out over the South Seas. They came out as a sort of archipelago, but passable nevertheless, and some day will make a fine harbour. I also oversaw the creation of some new varieties of birds and turtles on my new islands.

Dealing with prayers wasn't so much fun. Sometimes they were decidedly humdrum—like people asking for their onions and garlic to grow—and hardly needed a god to make happen. Others were outrageous or impossible, which no god could or would grant. Some were in conflict with each other, like the wish for one side or the other to win in battle, or the Olympic Games, so no god could satisfy everyone. But I came to realise that expectations were generally low, and I needed to do very little for at least someone or other to get their wish, sooner or later.

'I see you now have mastered divine intervention,' said Hermes. 'But come, let us stop talking shop; we have more important things to attend to.'

And so we headed off to dinner, which was located in something called the Gods' Mess. All around this celestial canteen was the contented hubbub of diners' conversation and godly tummies rumbling, and the gentle breaking of divine wind, and the aroma of heavenly cuisine. At the longest table you ever saw were all the gods you could think of. I spotted Ares arguing with Aphrodite, while Helios the sun god was talking very loudly to a bored-looking Eos, the god of dawn.

Hermes warned me that the provincial gods were always quarrelling with each other or else gossiping about other gods. Also, he admitted that the gods were not necessarily as good role models as might be imagined. I replied that it was okay, most people knew this already.

Hermes also explained that heaven is quite crowded these days, after it was opened up to admit all sorts of foreign and barbarian gods, as well as goddesses, hybrids and demi-gods, and even some gods from beyond Atlantis. Hence the extended Mess.

And so we joined the meal. I was seated amidst an exotic diversity of foreign gods—on my right was Mithras, a god from Persia, said to be born of a virgin. On my left, there sat Isis, a goddess from Egypt, and her son Horus, who have a cult of resurrection. Opposite was an Aztec god—also born of a virgin—and next to him, a Celtic goddess whose name I didn't catch, and next to her was a crocodile-headed god whose name I couldn't pronounce.

Soon enough, a grizzled Ganymede filling my cup with wine said conspiratorially, 'What do you think of this rabble?'

As a guest—and maybe a barbarian myself—I wasn't sure what to think, far less say. But Ganymede gave me his opinion anyway.

'See that Egyptian there—the dog-faced gentleman in the linen suit—who does he think he is? Does he expect to establish his divinity by barking? I mean, call me old-fashioned, but surely gods are gods, and dog-heads are dog-heads? Or see that guy with the caftan and cap? That's Mithras the Mede. He doesn't even speak Greek, so he can't even understand if you're praising or insulting him. And as for those freaks over there, heaven is simply *swarming* with these demi-gods.'

With that, he offered me some of Poseidon's sprats, and some strange-looking vegetables. 'Won't you try some lovely tomatls or avocadls?' said the Aztec god. 'Or treat yourself to some chocolatl?'

While the gods had historically only eaten ambrosia and drunk nectar, most gods nowadays had an eclectic palate including all sorts of vegetables and animal meats.

'Don't worry,' said the crocodile-headed god, with a hungry look in his eye. 'Human flesh is not on the menu, today.'

'We just inhale the savoury smoke of the sacrifices,' said the Aztec god.

It seemed that the gods were always having dinner, or supper, or breakfast, or lunch, or going to sleep. Each day always seemed to be a holy day or religious festival or sabbatical for one god or another.

I asked who got to become a god these days, and Zeus said I'd learn soon enough, as he was going to issue a judgment on that very matter, the next day.

So we then retired for the night. I didn't sleep much, as so many things were churning around in my head. For a start, I was puzzling about how there can be night in heaven when the Sun is always there, sharing their meals.

Next morning, Zeus called a council to proclaim about the constitution of the gods and admission to heaven.

'I have to report some complaints about the influx of so many foreign gods, hybrid gods, and demi-gods, at the expense of our more ancient and genuine gods. Heaven is becoming too noisy, too crowded, and it's pushing up the price of ambrosia and nectar.

'So here runs my judgement. First, all gods that have already been admitted shall be permitted to remain. After all, some of them have already assimilated, fallen in love and have families here. Besides, one of the great benefits of the diversity of gods is the great diversification of cuisine that has been opened up.'

It was true enough: it's almost impossible now to imagine going back to a heaven worthy of the name, lacking the foreign foods, especially those brought by the New World gods. The Roman gods would grumble without their *tricolore* salads, the Greek goddesses would miss their stuffed peppers, and the Britannic gods would be bereft without their fish dishes served with fried chipped potatls.

'Second, all gods will be required to learn Greek—although they may speak in their own tongues amongst themselves—as long as they do it quietly.

'Thirdly, as for demi-gods, we shall place a tighter rein on which offspring of the gods are deemed worthy of admittance. Those seeking admission must bring documentary proofs of their origin, and the reason and circumstances of their deification. Henceforth also there shall be a presumption against excessive procreation with mortals—gods should not presume they can copulate with humans with impunity. And there shall be outright prohibition of anyone of purely human origin entering heaven, unless a guest of a deity.'

I had not been contemplating copulating with a god with or without impunity. But the question of who might gain access to heaven was interesting as it related to philosophical debates back in the human realm.

'So, does this mean that ordinary mortals won't gain access to an afterlife in heaven?' I ventured.

'Humans, living in heaven?' The gods all fell about laughing. 'Where on earth did you get that idea?'

Zeus replied: 'I'm afraid that is a fantasy among some of the more deluded human cults. There's certainly no room for any mortals here—we're already stuffed to the gills with gods!'

At that, I shuffled a bit nervously, and thought it best to take my leave. I thanked Zeus for all his hospitality, but suggested it might be time to return to Earth.

'Yes, that is for the best,' Zeus replied. 'Moreover, we don't want more of your sort coming this way.' And just to be sure there would be no repeat of my unsolicited visit from below, they confiscated my wings.

And so I was carried back to Earth by Hermes, and dropped off in the Potters' Quarter in Athens. Before parting, I asked what I might tell of my adventure in Heaven—the manipulation of the weather, the exotic gods from lands beyond Atlantis, and rules for admittance to heaven?

'I'm sure you're free to say whatever you like,' said Hermes. 'But in my experience, it's always best to tell people only things they already know, or already suspect. It could be too shocking, otherwise. Some things they just won't want to hear; some things they just won't understand; and some things they just won't believe.

'And whatever you say, don't let people think there's any chance of coming to the heavens—whether alive or dead. So you should write up what happened as one of your True Stories—so no-one will believe a word of it.

The God-fatherer

The flight had become a white-knuckle ride of epic pro-portions. My fingers gripped the hand-rests as the plane listed and lurched in the turbulence. All around, faces ashen, people staring ahead, occasional wailing. Some people were praying, others crossing themselves. It's at times like this you remember how finely life hangs by a thread, and you wonder if you should have taken up religion as an insurance policy on your soul.

But the guy next to me seemed completely calm and serene about it.

He was classically tall, dark and handsome, with his bronze-grey skin, long face and strong nose, and side-burns of a style either hopelessly adrift of the fashion, or audaciously ahead of it. But he had a certain unearthly charisma about him that was strangely reassuring in these unusual circumstances.

He had been reading a book doggedly through the dimness of the cabin, as if he was in a time zone of his own, his otherwise solemn expression punctuated with the occasional smirk or tut. The book's cover showed what looked like a sultry, scantily clad pharaohess kneeling before a handsome bronzed male figure, who had a passing resemblance to the book's reader.

Seeking a distraction from our little airborne difficulty, I couldn't resist breaking the taboo of the silent intimacy of the cabin, to ask him what the book was.

He turned and looked at me as if for the first time, and spoke with a deep but gentle voice, enunciated with what I took to be a distant European accent: 'The book? Is about Egypt. Ancient Egypt. But it's a contemporary novel—an erotic novel, a classic example of god-porn.'

His reply was said in a straightforward manner—as if I should be expected to know what god-porn was. In fact, I reckon he had less embarrassment at having to reveal he was reading an erotic novel, than I had for having exposed him.

'Sorry, I didn't mean to pry…'

But he held his hand up in quiet protest, a gentle frown on his face.

'Not at all. To tell the truth, it is difficult to get hold of any books about the gods these days.'

'Is it?'

'If they're there at all, they won't be found under religion, but more usually under history, or mythology, or even something like "Body, mind and spirit".'

'Ah yes, all those books on angels and star signs…?'

'You do get the occasional erotic novel featuring a god. The airport bookshops are sometimes the best places. This one was supposed to be written by a woman for women, though I think it must have been written by a man—or god—under a false name. But I don't think it was a god. The sex scenes with the god are all written from a human point of view.'

'Uh-huh.'

Despite my customary indifference to religion, the idea of sexual relations between gods, or between gods and humans, instinctively pricked my curiosity. While such shenanigans were not entirely unheard of in respectable literature, they were usually reported as simple mechanical facts or genealogical *faits accompli*, rather than as part of a narrative of seduction, amatory craft or rite of passage, which somehow would have made divine encounter seem more real.

'The funny thing is, the novel only works because the modern reader finds it exotic—erotic—a spice of sacrilegious, forbidden pleasure. But the ancient Egyptian would just see it as an unremarkable temple assignation, a girl-meets-god kind of thing. The ritual stimulation of the god being as natural as, say, grilling him a goat.'

He spoke with such calm authority that I hardly registered the outlandish thrust of his conversation.

'Look, pleasuring a god is no more about kinky sex than drinking the blood of a demi-god is about the forbidden pleasure of divine cannibalism. If you see what I mean.'

Then, as if suddenly remembering his manners, he shook my hand. 'Delighted to meet you. You might know me by my Greek name, Hermes. I'm God of Commerce, by the way.'

I tried to digest what I thought he had just said.

'What kind of commerce?' I ventured weakly.

'All commerce.' And as he turned, his eyes pierced into mine. 'And I'm also bearer of dead souls, and messenger of the gods.'

~~~

The rhythmic jungle beat of the drum and bass music is pulsating in my eardrums. There's a mosh of bodies heaving and bobbing in the dark in front of the big bonfire. My heart is beating and my pulse is racing as I dance with abandon, a manic reveller in some crazed twenty-first century fertility dance.

And there, gyrating just inches in front of me, within touching distance, is my striking new companion. With a long thin ageless face, strong nose, high cheek bones and lively eyes, he had hooked my attention since I first saw him. He has a sort of waistcoat on, which makes him look like maybe a musician or bohemian dressing up a bit. He looks every bit a man of the world, as if he were confident of being, if necessary, the only man in the world.

We've been fitfully getting to know each other, through just-snatched snippets of conversation, mainly of music and beer, and the visceral thrill of the Beltane festival, a splurge of energy and spirit and cosmic vibe and earthly passion, and the alcoholic sense of occasion of the awakening of the pagan spring.

Finally tiring, we find a bench free and sit down with our beers to pause for breath. Here we are under the strange dark light of the night over Calton Hill.

'So, what brought you here?' He smiles invitingly, in a distant accent.

'I'm here with my friends. I'm in Edinburgh, on a sort of year out. Life experience, I suppose. How about you?'

'Oh, I just thought I'd check out the scene, you know. Edinburgh always does a good gig for the Beltane.'

I take a large swig of Bohemia's finest. I'm not accustomed to all this beer, but I reckon my alcohol intake is just right for the occasion. As if in reply, my drinking companion takes a correspondingly large glug of his Viking ale.

There seems to be a dart of attraction between us, right enough. So there must be possibility of love, or at least lust, between us, even at such short notice and in the dark. Maybe, tonight could be the night.

A little cool gust is our cue.

'A bit chilly, eh?'

'Yeah...'

'Shall we go somewhere, then?' he says, looking around. We both laugh, as we look around, as we're on the gravelly top of an exposed hill, with no conceivable 'somewhere' to be seen, other than the city itself, glittering below.

'We could go back to my flat—it's just down there—Pilrig. Is that okay for you?'

'Yeah, cool.' He grins, and sinks the rest of his ale in one smooth gulp.

Before we head off, I seek out my friends round the other side of the bonfire, and say a brief goodnight. They seem to have hooked up with a part-time Viking and some sort of amateur satyr. And they can't help noticing my new companion and exchange approving smirks at this handsome catch.

And off we go down the hill together, and he puts his jacket round my shoulders. As I put my hands in the pockets, I find a purse and compass in one, and a little airline-size bottle of wine in the other. He puts an arm round me, and we partly prop each other up as we dip down the stony path towards Picardy Place. We walk in a comfortable enough silence; I don't really want to press him on where he came from or who he really is, or want to reveal much more about myself. Tonight is strictly physical.

~~~

I was looking out the window of the plane, my eyes tracking the fluffy clouds below. Next to me, two inches away, was an adult male self-identifying as a god. Not the usual odd-bod, claiming to be God: but just one of the gods—this was new, right enough. Maybe he was some bored businessman, or clever college graduate who got his kicks by pretending to live in the classical world, and amused himself by bamboozling people who crossed his path. We were only just starting our descent, so I had time enough to kill. There was nothing much to see outside but the crimson glimmer of first light, curiously opaque and almost unearthly. So I thought I would humour him. I cleared my throat.

'So, you're a pagan god then?' I said as casually as I could, stifling a smile.

He seemed not at all fussed by the inquiry.

'I suppose you could put it that way, yes. I am one of the gods.'

'So what are the other gods then? Gods of love, war, that sort of thing?' Wondering if my limited knowledge of classical deities would run out before I could catch him out.

'Yes, that's right.' He paused and smirked. 'There are goddesses too.'

Just then, I became aware that his gaze was hovering over the open front of my top, and I gently drew my cardigan together.

'And do you have any, er, goddess friends?'

'Oh yes, of course. Do you have any gentlemen friends? Sorry, none of my business. Anyway, we are well behaved. Mostly.' His eyes glinted mischievously.

Despite his forward nature, I couldn't help feeling warmed rather than repelled by his almost gentlemanly flirting. He seemed so effortlessly charming; I suppose I was flattered by the attention. I was already imagining telling my friends of meeting this curious stranger, a bit out of the ordinary but by no means off-putting. Being seduced by a 'god' would be something of a novelty, after all.

'So, you hang out with the other gods—is that just the Greek gods, or is it all gods?'

'All gods…Black gods, white gods, multi-coloured gods, straight gods, gay gods, hermaphrodites. An orgy of gods! Think of the possibilities!'

I tried to take in this rainbow menagerie of deities, and what they could be getting up to above the clouds. And then thinking, well why wouldn't they?

Then there was a lurch as the plane touched down, and the roaring of the reverse thrust of the engines filled the cabin.

I composed myself, and got my bearings. Here, on a routine airline flight, with just this strange companion talking about gods.

'So—what about God then?'

'God?' He smiled, looking pleasantly puzzled, as if feigning ignorance.

'You know, as in: the one true God and all that?'

'One true God, you say?'

'So, you're saying that God is just one of the gods?'

'I'm saying *any* god is "just one of the gods", as you put it.'

We stood up. He was tall, and stooped slightly. Everywhere people were rummaging around with their bags from the lockers. He put on a wide brimmed hat and said, 'I have to get off this plane.' He said it as if he were somehow acting independently of everyone else who were also naturally disembarking now.

'Aha, right, so you admit the God of the Bible does exist, then?'

He gave a scornful snort of laughter.

'Yahweh? An awful little god!'

'But isn't he respected and feared and…Almighty?'

I was in danger of becoming the devil's advocate for God.

'Ugh, no. He's way over-rated. He's a loner, a weirdo, a troublemaker. No-one likes him.'

'But you don't deny his existence?'

'I don't deny or acknowledge his existence any more than he denies or acknowledges ours, like when he says "Worship me not all those other gods." If we didn't exist, why would he say that?'

'But I thought no-one believed in the pagan gods any more.'

'On the contrary, there is a resurgence in belief in the gods.'

'Just because some people believe in those gods doesn't mean they exist?'

'Well, can you give a better reason?'

~~~

Heading down Leith Walk, we swing into the Deep Sea Fish and Chicken, and grab take-aways of hot battered fish and deep fried potatoes, then wend our way to my flat, eating our protein and calorific suppers as we walk and talk. I fumble with my key at the street door, and we stagger up the stairs in a half embrace, swaying together up three flights of steps to the top floor. Then I fumble again with the keys of my flat, and finally we're inside. Phew.

I say, 'Shh! My flatmates might be asleep.' We're soon in my bedsit and I close the door gratefully behind us.

He closes in on me, so I feel his touch.

'Is been a while,' he says with a sort of sheepish smile. 'Since being with a woman…'

'Me too,' I say, 'I mean—' Laughing nervously.

Then I tear myself away from him, to pour him a whisky—a large one for good measure. Let's put some music on—what? Let's see, lets' see… Too late to be cool now. Whatever's in the CD player will do for now. Red Hot Chilli Peppers. I switch to Björk, there we go. Go to the loo, the music echoing from the other room. Then to the kitchen, and knock back a shot of Cointreau. For relaxation and de facto painkiller, just in case. Then another dose, for luck. Come back. He's already lying naked spreadeagled on the bed. Well, it is a bedsit after all.

I turn off the light, and strip, and then he's all over me, like a shapeshifting alien, all fingers and thumbs and slithery limbs and tentacles tight round me and into me, as I grasp the miracle of our anatomical compatibility.

'They say men are from Mars, and women from Venus,' I say, not sure I really mean anything.

'Ground control to Major Tom.' He grins back, not meaning anything at all.

And I feel a giddy tingling fulfilment to be finally intimate with the male of the species.

~~~

Once inside the terminal, my god-talking companion and I were soon enough in the baggage hall, with a background chatter of passengers broken by odd disembodied announcements on the public address system. We stared blankly at the empty conveyor as it creaked and trundled round, and my mind went round and round thinking about my newly enlarged perspective on the gods.

I found my companion's point of view not wholly convincing, but yet tantalising and even seductive, liberating. It somehow helped make more sense of where

'God' fitted in to the wider divine realm: if you admit there being the possibility of supernatural beings such as gods, then it would be no less implausible, and indeed less exceptional, to have many gods rather than just the one, ever.

And it suddenly seemed more realistic and satisfying for there to be a variety of gods with different characters and behaviours, rather than just the one monopoly god to be lumbered with, such that godliness must be forever defined by a particular individual deity's historical faux pas, falling outs, tantrums, disasters, and ongoing demands for praise and sacrifice—rather than simply keeping the world ticking over, or bringing fertility or some other useful service, like the pagan gods.

And so, despite myself, I picked up again on our conversation. Well, if I changed the subject, it would mean either having to show renewed interest in him, or give away something about myself.

'So what about Jesus?'

'Ha,' he says, almost wincing. 'The undead demigod! I wondered if someone would ask. But I'm sure everyone knows the story. Gods on their travels have their needs, after all. And they—we—are anatomically compatible with human women. Well, despite all of Zeus' rule-making, sooner or later someone is going to get pregnant. Nice girl, already engaged. What a mess.'

The bags were now out and trundling around the carousel.

'So you're saying that one of the world's major religions was started by a, well, family planning accident?'

'An almighty fuck-up, basically.' He laughed somewhat bitterly at his own punchline, which I had set up for him. 'The less said the better.'

I had never really thought about it, that despite—or because of—the pagan connotations of demi-gods, Jesus' conception and birth made more sense in a pagan context than an Abrahamic one; indeed the world's most popular religion was in effect founded by a supernatural human-god hybrid love-child.

We hauled our bags off the carousel.

'So are you jealous of Jesus's popularity?' I teased.

'Why should I, son of Zeus, be jealous of Jesus?' he scoffed. 'Demi-gods are ten a penny these days. Any deity can make themselves popular if they promise something now that they're never going to have to deliver in the hereafter.

'Ah, but the mortals are a fickle bunch,' he sighed, and looked me in the eye, for once betraying an undercurrent of emotion. 'They don't really care for the gods at all. No, all they care for is themselves. They use us. All that devotion and piety and worship, but in the end it's all about what they can get out of it. They claim loyalty and offer supplication. But someone gives a better deal, and they follow someone else. Look at the Egyptian gods—worshipped, fed, clothed. Indulged, pleasured.

For thousands of years, and then abandoned as if they had never existed.'

'Or people get bored with the heavenly father, and follow the son?' I venture.

'Yeah, I suppose. So don't worry: we can look after ourselves just fine. Old gods don't really die; they just come back in some other guise. They call some of us angels; others, devils. And there's a whole new generation of people out there—wannabe believers in something or someone—just waiting to hook up with us.'

'Uh-huh?'

'Absolutely. Guess where I'm going now? The Beltane fire festival, in Edinburgh. A good old-fashioned gathering of the gods, with a massive bonfire, live sound system, and plenty of beer.'

Though still a bit sceptical of his schtick, I couldn't fault his enthusiasm.

And it dawned on me that if you were going to cast your lot in with the supernatural, with all the attendant irrationalities, inconsistencies and implausibilities, you may as well get all the benefits available: worship your own heroes, groove to your own kind of music, and follow your own moral path, rather than rely on the historical accidents and inhibitions of just one tribe, one tradition.

Or put another way, if you have to believe six impossible things before breakfast, it may as well be an appetising breakfast. Not the same old set menu of rancid bacon, congealing eggs and overdone toast every day, but a whole buffet of possibility. Preferably, cruelty-free and not bad for your own health or well-being.

We had reached the point where our paths would diverge, as he was headed for European transfers, I was off to long haul.

He gave me his card, which read 'Hermes. God of Commerce. Annunciator. Disseminator.' Just before he disappeared, he said, 'Oh, I nearly forgot. Would you like to have my book?'

'Is that the one about the god porn? Okay, thanks, I suppose I could give it a go. For research purposes, obviously.'

'Sure. It could get you in the mood for getting to know the gods. And you never know, today's god porn could be tomorrow's gospel.'

~~~

I wake up with a most awful headache, a roaring ringing hangover. I must have slept deeply, like the sleep of the dead. Ashtrays, and cigarettes that I don't remember smoking all over the place. An abandoned bottle of Cointreau. Memories of the night before, hazy flashbacks in disordered instalments.

And recollections of the weirdest dreams.

An undead demi-god in a chip shop serving deep sea chickens, red hot chilli peppers and god sauce. Then a three-headed dog-god wolfing down a human kebab and tricolore salad. And another dream, about wilfully seducing and ravishing an anatomically correct pagan god posing as an angel with sideburns.

And now groggily coming to on a wreck of a bed, with the pungent smell of sweat and who knows what all over the sheets and headboard, and the vaguely disturbing thought of having unprotected sex with an itinerant deity.

Belying his angelic alter-ego, and presumed experience, he was somewhat clumsy and even crude in his consummation. It was all over more quickly than I expected. But the deed was done. Before my year was up, for better or worse, my new flame Gabriel delivered me from my virginity.

Celestial Civil Service Blues

I'm not really a 'people person'; never was. Oh, I've known anthropologists, and some social workers. But that's not really my scene. All those awful people, their aches and pains and grumbles. And the smell. I still attend the occasional Judgement. But it's very messy. Flesh everywhere. Ugh.

You should see their faces when they arrive. It's as if they'd never given eternity a moment's thought. The shock, of having to serve. Get stuff done. Work, of different sorts. Some sing, sure. Yeah, and some man the latrines. Some stoke the fires. Community service. Celestial messengers, escorts, heavenly hostesses. Bar work, paperwork: it's still work. For gods' sakes, what do they expect? We all have to work. 'But I want to meet my Maker!' they plead. Yeah, well, join the queue.

I mean, they're never happy in their skins. Sure, they've heard of reincarnation. So they shouldn't expect to have their original bodily forms. I mean, what do they need genitals for? As if they're expecting to spend the end of their days pleasing themselves.

Or they imagine arriving and just sprouting a pair of wings. But there are wings and wings. They never seem to imagine an afterlife singing the praises of their god as a canary; or a cockroach.

The looks on their faces when they realise their true place in the scheme of things. Well, what did you expect? We have *dominion* over you. That means frankly that you are at our *disposal*. You should see the shock, when they realise they're to be fattened for the table, or made into glue.

~~~

Applications, applications. So much hope, so much desperation. So many, simply not good enough, simply unsuitable. Oh dear. Some are really chancing their arm, others are special pleading. But no. You, sir, are toast. And you—to the pit! And you, madame, the lake of fire. And *mademoiselle*, well, the grappling-hooks await your tender parts.

The Book of Life is in my hands. At my fingertips. We have the data. The low-down. All the names, the fingerprints, the genetic profiles, the works. An image of each soul. So it goes, it falls to me to edit the Book, to enter and to delete entries. Whoops, there goes Mrs. Chris Christopoulos. Good intentions, but Not Good Enough. The tragedy of the human condition.

I mean, some gods are so choosy, even about who's allowed to worship them. One god I worked for, he wouldn't accept bread offerings from those he considered inferior. The blind, the lame, the deformed or disfigured. The crooked-backed. Dwarves. People with bad skin condition, or crushed testicles. I mean, that's a god being fussy just about accepting offerings *from* the punters. So you can imagine, they're even more choosy about those who are to *be* the sacrifice.

Only the purest are selected, of course. Cleanliness is next to godliness and all that. Moral cleanliness, I should say. If you've had a good pure life, well, it just *feels* right and proper—though I'm not sure it really affects the flavour.

Most don't make the grade, of course. And really, telling us you like playing the piano is really not going to help much, Mr Jimmy Jesus Díaz. But still, there is usually room for a few more cockroaches in the chorus.

It's just as well we don't give too much away in advance. If they knew the truth, all hell would break loose.

~~~

Committees, committees. I've done my share of committee work. The Ethics Committee, the Karma Committee, the Purgatory Committee. Nearly ten years on the Taxonomic Committee. Minute this, minute that. Details, details. Endless debates on beetles. Decisions, decisions. At least in the old days it was *big* issues that made a *difference*. Are bats birds? When's a fish not a fish? When it's a shellfish. Or a papally enabled capybara. Deary me. That one went all the way up to the Head of Vertebrates.

Still, it all needs administration. The legal department is always poring over some technicality to do with bestiality or vegetarianism. Some anatomical slip-up or fashion faux pas or culinary cock-up. And the paperwork for Acts of Gods can be horrendous. Gomorrah versus Yahweh still has reverberations.

Still, it's better than the old days. It was anarchy then. They made up the rules as they went along—what else would they do? So you could mate with your mother—father a child with her—and that was, apparently, fine. But if you so much as looked at your brother's daughter, you could be done to death before death had even been diagnosed, never mind murder made a crime.

But we take Ethics very seriously now. Second only to welfare, actually. Not to forget health and safety, obviously. The biggest debate in ethics is always about *how* you take the life. Even the gods can't agree amongst themselves. Is it more ethical to have your subjects killed ritually in advance, while they are alive on Earth, and fully aware of what is happening to them, surrounded by their own people? Or is it better to take 'em unawares, their souls served up to the gods live, hot and thrashing?

~~~

The Celestial Civil Service runs everything these days. Yes, we used to have proper gods; I mean, gods with balls, who had real powers. But all the real work is done by the Service now.

We have to keep a sense of balance between the needs of the people and the needs of the gods. It was always thus. If you concede too much to the people, the gods get stroppy. And the people never know what they really want. They don't know what to do with their freedom; there is general anarchy; and people appeal to the gods again, wanting stronger authority, yet mightier Almighties.

Then again, if you give too much power to the gods, it's counter-productive, as the punters feel overburdened, with onerous rituals, unrealistic demands, and they either just ignore them, or start to rebel, or shift their allegiance to some other god offering easier terms.

But don't blame us. Whatever we do, we just do the paperwork, in the name of the gods. Though all the gods and paper in the world are meaningless, unless the punters themselves go along with it.

I mean, people are so deferential; they accept being at God's whim; do anything to get to Heaven, on any terms, happy to be completely at God's disposal. It's the people who put up with all this crap. No wonder we get contemptuous, capricious, complacent deities. You get the gods you deserve.

~~~

Gods, gods, don't talk to me about gods. So many mad gods, bad gods, dangerous-to-know gods. I've seen them all in my time. Some are workaholics. Some are masochists. Most are misogynists. Some are a danger to themselves. They get quoted out of context, or caught with their trousers down. And it's us who have to clean up the mess.

We try to keep the gods away from social media. Save them from themselves. They'd only start to share pictures of their private parts. Besides, they think their importance is proportional to how much they say, how often. They'd just repeat endless platitudes and pass on praise about themselves; or say something controversial, incite violence and hatred. Oh wait…

The gods have such high opinions of themselves. Even if they're responsible for the *tiniest* thing, they're still the god of it. The god of travel passes, for example. Or tin openers. Or fridge lights. You'd think those weren't the most crucial things in the world. And yet… millions upon millions of fridges. Billions, even. All that food, needing illumination. Think about it. All those midnight snacks. You wouldn't want any to go to waste—all those frustrated vegetables and futile carcasses. Someone has to be responsible for the mess… Who else, but a god?

But you have to tread carefully sometimes. Remember, the gods have their popular mandate, their personal fanbase, and don't they know it. They boast about the number of their followers; and how fanatical their worshippers are. Gods gadding about, posing as angels to seduce virgins. As if a mortal could conscionably give consent.

You'll hear loads of gossip about your God. Oh yes. It's usually said very discreetly, of course. His personal life is more or less out of bounds. Even hinting at his having a personal life is a no-no.

You need to be careful how to address him. We all know the drill though. Some things go without saying. You never address him by his personal name, but simply 'God'. Other acceptable terms are 'Lord' and 'Almighty'. You can even say things like 'O Great One' (He knows who you mean). Just, don't sound sarcastic.

~~~

I suppose I was not cut out to be a god. I admit, I used to be envious of them, just a little bit. You know, run everything, issue commands, accept worship, invent rituals, that sort of thing. Go among your people. Create things. Invent improbable animals. Play with the weather. Change the course of battles. Destroy cities. Or move them to a different part of the world.

And all the trappings. The expense account. The holidays. A room to yourself, with a window facing the light, and a proper name plaque on your door. And of course, the biographies.

I've been there, seen it all first hand. I've had my time in all the hifalutin departments. I shadowed an archangel once. Knew the God, personally. I was an extra in one of his films.

But I'm not bitter, no. Looking back, I came to realise it wasn't being a god, as such, that I actually wanted. Rather, it was the power that went with it. After all, it's us who decide what the gods say and do. It's us who issue the commandments, write the press releases, and fabricate the back stories.

Some say it's a cushy number—a nice metaphysical desk job, office hours, a decent pension in perpetuity. But while the hours may be fixed, the ratio of people to gods always increases; and your work's never done. You hardly get time to treat cases properly; sometimes you have to deal with applications or judgements in job lots. The administrative equivalent of a mass grave. But the work itself is agreeable enough, if you have an eye for detail, a tidy mind, and just the right blend of caring, casual and callous. As humane as humane can be, one might say.

I've worked on some serious legislation in my time. The most important laws concern relations between the gods, of course. I've worked on the cases about harmonising relations between different gods from different jurisdictions; who is qualified to be a god; and relations with mortals. Yes, that's the power of the Service behind the scenes. In many ways it's us who decide who the gods really are. The gods always say that without them, we'd be nothing. But I always reckon it's the other way around.

~~~

The new gods—or goddesses, it's all the same—are the worst. They come in with their righteous anger and radical new ideas, and start trying to throw their weight around. It's all very well having some fresh blood, but you have to have some sort of continuity, stability; and the rules must actually work.

The new gods, they sometimes look down on us, at first. But soon they cotton on. At least, the smart ones do. The ones who don't get it, they are soon floundering. It's a bit embarrassing. Without proper administrative support, a god can be exposed, undermined, humiliated. Hung out to dry. Excoriated. Flayed. Fisted. Snuffed out. Or worse.

Yes, worse: without proper PR, they lose the attention of the people. People stop tuning in, or reading their press releases any more. They are ignored, forgotten, abandoned. All their authority drains away; they become gods in name only, little more than figures of speech, filed away under mythology.

As I say, the new gods sometimes look down on us, when they first arrive. They think we are inferior, as if we don't have our own god-like qualities. They think we are just petty pen-pushers, as if it's the gods who do the real action, and we don't know anything about the so-called real world. But we have done more training than they have. We know more about people, and certainly more about religion, than they do. To say nothing of history, anthropology, laws, languages, you name it.

And then there's the practical. A whole Earth year on the ground. You get a sense of what it's like to be mortal all right, living dangerously, living for the moment. Phew. You have to walk in their shoes for a bit, drag yourself over the land in their lumpen bodies. Clomp, clomp. See the world through eyes of gristle.

~~~

Life, death, afterlife… the whole mortality gig seems to be the hardest thing for the punters to figure. I mean they mouth the words as if they do get it. They say that when someone dies they are personally being called at a time of God's choosing, and they are off to be at one with God. But I see it more like your favourite fish restaurant, with the tank of live fish, and there's Florence swimming around, no wait it's Hortense, no, wait, how about that big fat one, yes, that one, you'll do. Then suddenly poor old Alphonse is scooped up, cut down like a flower—no, cut down like a fish, more like—metaphysically filleted and stir-fried and on the table within minutes. Now your soul is truly at one with the godhead—or god-gut—dissolved, digested, washed down with a nice rosé.

~~~

Yes, to your God, you are simply 'human resources'. At best, you're kept like a domestic pet, left to graze in heavenly ignorance. At worst, you're worked to death doing dirty, dangerous jobs. At any rate, you're more like livestock than one of your God's own Children.

I mean come on, when you look at the gods' *actual* children, that's more the picture—the spoilt so-and-sos, with their halos and magic powers and special privileges, getting to swan around all the domains as they please, groomed as partners in the family business. In hindsight, it was a mistake to hint that people of dust might ever be part of God's actual family.

But the gods still care for your welfare, oh yes. After all, who wouldn't want their flock to have a happy life? But then, when you have dominion, you hold all the cards, and call the shots. You subdue them all right: rear them, shear them, brand them, dock them, neuter them, stuff them, then butcher them. Dominion: disposal. Whatever and whenever suits you.

I'm pretty sure your God loves you, well, as far as He's God, and you're walking dead meat. The Good Shepherd is, after all, the Grim Reaper. I daresay you love your lambs, before you slaughter them. But then you just love *lamb*.

No wonder all the nervous rumours up and down the queue to the afterlife. What if the light is blinding? Maybe only those with wings get to sing. They say the only balls are gods' balls.

~~~

Some say the Service is full of failed gods. I prefer to see it the other way around—that the Pantheon is full of failed civil servants. A bunch of would-be control freaks who don't have the skill or dedication to actually control anything.

The Godheads are just figureheads now, largely ceremonial. They are wheeled out with the robes, the raiment, the laurels, the golden phalluses, the funny handshakes, the smoke and mirrors. Yet what good do they actually do for the average punter? Most of the time, you may as well have an AI chatbot for a deity. At least a godbot gives the semblance of listening, and their answers make as much sense, for all the difference it makes.

Of course, the odd noble god or charismatic individual can occasionally carry the day. But it's us who do the real work, who make things tick, who get things done. And the great masses of regulations have to be worked out somewhere, ground out in the wheels of the Celestial Civil Service, not the soundbites of some jumped-up deity. Sorry, guys. Call me cynical, but there you go.

We have to stick to the script, more or less. But there is some leeway. The skill is to make the divine hegemony seem the natural order; for the rules to be as unobtrusive as possible, as if they were their own, so the hand of the bureaucrat is not seen at all. But be careful who you tell, obviously, in case they get the idea that there's no need for gods in the first place. And then where would we be?

~~~

Some people really seem to dread the gods, and rant against them, as if the gods are tyrants over them. But I just laugh at that. Some gods couldn't tie their own shoe laces. I mean, literally. Some gods lost their balls a long time ago. Their tongues, too.

No, it's not gods that people should fear, but people— who just use gods as a front for human tyranny. In truth, you don't even need any gods to run your theocracy. All you need for hell is other people.

Even gods should fear their fate in human hands. Did you hear the one about the god who tried to come back as a human? They tortured him to death.

Bedtime @ The Goddess'

On the way back from a squat party south of Market, our heads are filled with wild colourful music ringing in our ears, machine-raging and jungling grunge Amen-breaking together as if heralding a new musical fusion future. The winds of change are blowing across the Bay, breathing in a new age of insurgent technology and cyberpunk possibility. I find myself bundled in the back of a cab, squeezed in next to Jim, and lying half on top of this striking looking girl with black eyeliner, a long velvety dress and lots of jingly-jangly jewellery.

The taxi swerves round a final San Francisco corner and we slump together in a pile as it pulls up at someone's apartment on Lower Nob Hill.

Behind an unassuming façade, a place of esoteric individuality opens up, past the psychedelic beads and dreamcatcher charms, the waft of incense and drapes with signs of the zodiac, and etchings of crows and vultures and sphinxes.

I excuse myself to the bathroom. It's done out in matt black, with little painted stars and moon symbols, as if I'd stumbled into a time-warped celestial closet. On the way back I can't resist a peek into one of the bedrooms, which is full of images of gothic revelry, naked cat-headed women and Egyptian-looking gods and goddesses.

In the main room, flatmates and guests are loafing around on beanbags, squatting on the wooden floor, smoking tobacco and pungent roll-ups and noisily knocking back tequilas and beers.

And there in the middle of the room, holding court like a black widow spider in the centre of her web, there is the striking velvety woman, our hostess, who is channelling the universal 'Goddess'.

'I'm a proper grown-up god. With an adult agenda. None of your Santa Clauses or make-believe redeemers. I am not your social worker. I deal serious stuff, about you and me. I am the Goddess of love, of lust, fertility, fecundity, full frontal fucking nudity, experimental sexual chemistry and self-fucking-discovery.

'I am the Goddess's Goddess; the Creatrix-Dominatrix; Mistress of the Universe. I can be who you want me to be. Come to me, through me, for love, succour, discipline or supplication, and the path to sexual satisfaction.'

'So, what does a Goddess of Sex actually do?' says Euan, a particle physicist, matter-of-factly, more used to the unrealities of the quantum world than the spiritual entanglements of humanity and divinity.

'I empower you to avail of your own sexuality,' says the Goddess.

'Why do we need a Goddess for that?' says Euan.

'To fill a hole, so to speak, left by the religion you thought you'd got shot of, but which still leaves you thinking sex is something furtive or dirty, rather than something your Maker loves you for, and does for Herself.'

'I didn't realise there was such a demand for goddesses in the Bay Area,' says Leon, a Silicon Valley empiricist, just when tech was on the cusp of cool.

'Listen, most of history has been Goddess-worshipping,' she explains. 'The Goddess line is older and grander than any rabble of Babylonian bible bashers. Preacher men rant and rave against me while pretending I am not there. But it seems they protest too much against someone who they say doesn't exist. For thousands of years, goddesses of all shapes and sizes—mothers, daughters, sisters, witches, lovers—have been available for worship and satisfying your need for divine Love, of a feminine kind. My good works are everywhere. Otherwise, my friends, you would not be here,' she says, looking round at her audience.

'I've been on the scene—or just behind the scenes—for as long as history can recall. Though they did their best to write us out of it. But you can read me between the lines. I am the dark star, who you can tell by the wobble I induce in others.

'I was famed—notorious—in the lives of the Israelites. Book after book of their bloody bible, generation after generation, ranting against false gods, preaching abstinence but all the while having a bit of me on the side.

'You never stopped to wonder why those naughty Israelites kept straying from their self-righteous, hectoring Lord? Maybe because those other gods offered a fuller package of sexual fulfilment as well as spiritual love, rather than the lectures of a jealous celibate, who preached that sex was sinful—which is about as fucked up as you can get. But I, the timeless, universal Goddess, was able to offer good deep loving sex as a path to spiritual fulfilment. Those were the days: I seduced King Solomon; satisfied Goliath; drove God to distraction.'

Something tells me this is not going to be the usual mindless human being getting-to-know-you chit-chat kind of night.

~~~

Life as a goddess can be tough. For a start, getting any sort of official recognition is a nightmare—your title, pronouns, tax status in different jurisdictions…even the image for your photo ID. It's not that I'm so vain, but a Goddess of Love has to be sexy. Or at least, look the part. You have to make sure this goddess really has the look of Love—and not of Agriculture, for example, or Accounts.

My website is my main medium, my own online Temple of Love. I offer spirituality, meditation, dream interpretations, and love energy therapy, and a sexual healing chat line. You could say I use the pleasures, practicalities and hang-ups of sex as a lure to unlock people's spirituality, and spirituality to deepen and season their appreciation of sex. And I do a side-line in mail order aphrodisiacs and sex accessories.

My clients and followers are not primarily lonely hearts, or horny punters looking for a hook-up. After all, there's no shortage of dating agencies or strings-free sex on the world wide web. But people sometimes want more than that. They crave a missing link between body, mind and spirit: a philosophy that fits with the beliefs they already hold. We reach out to everyone who has normal modern views on love and sex, and who seek some kind of spiritual connection, but who would never be seen dead in a church.

I draw from familiar traditions of building religious movements. If you want to gain a following, you must be open to anyone. Don't make it too hard to join—but make people feel special for joining in. Don't make the rituals too difficult, painful or tiresome. Don't make too many impossible things to believe before brunch. Better still, align yourself with what people already believe, and give them things they can actually have, in this life. Bring a fresh perspective, but draw on wisdom from more ancient traditions.

I wasn't immediately a natural at this game. At first, my public persona was quite cautious, self-conscious, even defensive; but I soon got into the swing of things, found my voice, got bolder, but less preachy; I'm more likely to laugh off an argument with a roll of the eyes than pull rank, or quote chapter and verse.

And I like the combination of accessibility and anonymity that online offers. I can appear to be out there and reaching into your room, but I get to stay in my own private space. I project an official image, but no-one knows what I really look like. I suppose that's a prerogative of any deity. I give hints, of course. But my fondest followers will picture me with straggly, imperfectly dyed grey hair, half-dressed in old worn tracksuit bottoms, as I slum around my dusty old house in Baja California, posting little soundbites of Love on my website, with a roll-up hanging out my mouth, and a glass of red wine, listening to an old Alanis Morrissette album.

I guess no-one would have imagined this is how or where I would end up. But here I am. With a little help from my techie friends Leon and Euan, my online station is up and running. Whether it's live chat, podcasts or private sexual healing, you can access my services 24/7 at Bedtime@TheGoddess'.

~~~

It had never occurred to me that I might end up spending the night with a Goddess of Sex—though I'd never ruled it out either. It all came about quite accidentally, as we were to leave the rest of the party and go into The Goddess' room, to look at her esoteric books on new age paganism, and play her music. With nowhere to sit, Jim crashes out on her giant-sized bed, and I perch on the opposite corner. And then our resident Goddess plumps herself down voluptuously between us.

'There's always room for bedtime at the Goddess,' says the Goddess.

Our hostess gives off a kind of Cleopatra vibe, part Hellenic, partly African, but mixed in with a gothic neo-pagan look somehow conjuring a combination of Californian hippy chick and old-world high priestess of sex, with a twist of Bay Area savvy.

'So, how did you come to be an actual Goddess?' says Jim, ever the literalist.

'It was a gradual metamorphosis, I suppose. I had drifted for a while, a de facto agnostic. As a rebellious teenager, I tried believing in nothing, but lapsed. I guess I just had this hankering that there was more to life than atoms in the void. So I was drawn back to some kind of spirituality, and the appeal of living divinity.

'So, are you saying you're like the spirit of an ancient but ongoing Goddess?' says Jim.

'Yes, I channel the living Goddess; I *am* the living Goddess.'

'How can you be a goddess and human too?' says Jim.

'I see it like this. There is spark of divinity within us all; so it's possible to harness this, be your own goddess. This divinity transcends us, flows through us, so continues after we're gone… So why not acknowledge this divinity within, rather than denying it, as if it belongs to someone else, or neglecting it as a sort of other-worldly life-force that we only access when we're dead?'

'Hmm,' says Jim. 'So, are you your own religion?'

'Not exactly. But as the Goddess of my own belief, I can believe in what I like from veganism to free love...'

'How do you combine the Goddess bit—the religion—with the Love bit? Is it like a theological excuse for sex?'

'Nah, sex doesn't need an excuse. I see it as natural, good and pure as it is; not either something dirty to be suppressed, or some tired old animal habit needing spicing with the frisson of sin.

'I see myself not just a Goddess of Sex, but an all-round sensual spiritualist. And a seductress of strait-laced atheists,' she says, looking at Jim. 'And queer-laced ones too,' she adds, her gaze now alighting on me, almost as if noticing me for the first time.

~~~

You get all sorts on here—restless, hot-mess housewives, their sex-hungry sons, closet Cleopatras out in the sticks, hipsters looking for a holy fix. Self-lovers and self-loathers; lonely guys looking for someone to lose their roadhouse blues. Then there are the religious types—and angry atheists—who can't accept sexuality and spirituality being tangled up, or who can't bear others having a good time.

Sometimes I get this guy who claims to be God. An international caller, he tends to ramble on about the iniquities of evil men and seductresses and idolatresses. Imagine what this guy must be like at home—some grumpy family man with a sapphic Egyptian fixation.

'Caller, what's your point?'

'Hello? Is that you peddling your irreligious filth again?'

'There's nothing irreligious about sexual love...'

'What, so says the "Goddess of Love"? Are you some sort of erotic temptress, lady? If you are a lady, that is. And not a WHORE.'

'Only an erotic temptress if you'd like me to be, big boy. No shame in being a sex worker, by the way. It beats being a fucking wanker. I pity you. You see sexual depravity everywhere, but aren't getting any. But in case you hadn't noticed, tiger, the title "God of Love" was already taken...'

'Oh right then who's that then, some unholy online Gigolo?'

'You've never heard of the God of Love?'

Some of these guys, I think their bark is worse than their bite. It's just that anonymity makes them bolder than if we knew who they were in real life.

'I am The LORD GOD.'

'So you say, sir. But you're welcome, we engage with all faiths and none. Whatever floats your theological boat...'

'Well, what makes you think that I AM not indeed the one true eponymous LORD GOD?'

'If you were really the eponymous sodding LORD GOD, why would you be hanging around talking to an online goddess of love at this ungodly hour, hmm?'

'I could ask the same of you—why would a true Goddess choose to expose herself to the riff-raff?'

'Riff-raff, like you? Well, why wouldn't a goddess go among her people? Anyway, let's not argue again about Who's Who, or if there's a Deity in our midst. After all, how's anyone to know when a God starts—or stops—talking?'

~~~

At some point during the night, Jim must have got up and found somewhere else to crash. The three of us was either too much for him, or not enough. But it means that I end up, by chance, spending the night alone with the Goddess of Sex.

Nothing too much happens, physically. But psychologically, it turns out to be transformative. The sexual self-confidence of the Goddess seems to seep into me. As we stare up at the ceiling, which is covered in little luminous stars, the Goddess reveals her secrets in a husky whisper.

'Sex is our birthright; it's essentially designed to be enjoyed,' she says. 'They say God made the vagina; but the Goddess gave us our clitoris…es.'

She shifts and sits a bit more upright as if to make a wider point.

'As I see it, sexual pleasure comes from within; and so it doesn't really matter who or what turns you on. I'm all for free love—same sex, hetero sex, solo sex—for everyone. Even the ancient religions could accept different kinds of love. Take the Egyptians, they even had a place at the top table for sexually ambiguous gods and goddesses. Think of Atum—the great He-She as a divine role model, with male and female parts. There's nothing better to blow away the cobwebs of traditional religion than believing the world was created by a masturbating hermaphrodite.

'I'd rather believe that the great Creator hand-shandied the world into existence, than he was a cruel misogynist who made periods painful and child-bearing dangerous on purpose.'

'Well, when you put it like that…' I say.

'So, as I see it, it's not religion that's the problem, but the wrong kind of religion. Who says religion needs to be a totalitarian patriarchy, with one guy at the top who makes all the rules? So we're like naughty kids forever under the thumb of the headmaster? Why not be a collective, like a book-reading group, or internet forum, where everyone can have an opinion? Or just do your own thing, in private?

'I mean, people like Jim may say there is no such thing as gods or spirituality, and sex is just an amoral mechanical act. Perhaps it is for Jim. But it needn't be for you and me. I prefer to see sex as positively good, and moral: something the gods approve of and encourage. I am drawn to seek religions that can give me that.'

She is particularly fascinated by the ancient religions of Greece and Egypt, where gods and goddesses were not disinterested abstractions, filtered through the dark ages; but behaved like flesh and blood people, with real needs and urges.

'I mean, they looked good, wore sexy clothes, practically made god porn an art form, got drunk, had drunken sex too, with mortals and each other.'

'But free love and holiness are strange bedfellows, no?' I say.

'Only if you were unlucky enough to have been repressed since childhood by a religion dominated by celibate men, projecting the hang-ups of a hopelessly asexual god.'

'But—'

'Not that there's anything wrong with being ace, by the way; the problem was always sexuality or asexuality imposed by others.

'For many religions—most religions for all I know—deities come in male and female varieties. So for many, sex is something that gods and goddesses approve of and indulge in themselves. I mean, they had genitals and made love: why else are there both gods *and* goddesses?'

The question hangs in the air, as we think of something else to say.

'You know, I once met a guy called Hermes on a plane,' she says. 'I think he fancied me. And that's where I got my first affinity with the gods.'

'And does the Goddess have any Gods in her life now?' I ask her gently.

She looks back over her shoulder, and I see a glint of streetlight—or is it starlight—in her eyes.

'Gods, no. But then, I haven't been with a Goddess for a while, either…'

~~~

I could've been a pagan goddess, yes, with big nipples and a bulging crotch. Isis had her strong points—as mother and lover—but just a little too close to being a Madonna. Artemis, Ishtar, Bendis… they all had some sort of appeal. And any number of Celtic goddesses. Many goddesses and One Goddess.

I tried several personas, but none really fitted. I could identify with goddesses of the past, but only up to a point. Turns out they were not all sweetness and light. Some were amoral or downright immoral, like any old god with earthly power. Some were too abstract, or otherworldly, or too fixated with arcane or extinct rituals.

And to be honest, I missed some of the old-fashioned humanity of my own tradition.

But it turned out that paganism provided a catalyst to a new way of thinking—and not just for me. An old flame, Jim, who I'd never managed to win over, seems to be flirting with polytheism these days. He reckons polytheism is an easier bedfellow to live with for the non-believer than a single monotheistic god. It seems he has mellowed a bit, no longer just a straitlaced atheist. Reckons he's now more of a *poly*atheist. Like, an atheist, but in a context of polytheism: not as an angry outlier in opposition to everyone, but a humbler punter in the throng, in sync with any and all who ever disbelieved in anyone else's god. I hear he's now shacked up with a pagan systems analyst on Lower Nob Hill, so all's well that ends well.

I guess paganism can be like a prism, which can deflect the way you think about religion, in new ways. For someone like Jim, polytheism opened up a new spectrum of possibility, even if he ended up choosing none of the gods on offer.

For me, the prism of polytheism jolted me out of the easy assumptions of the past, and helped me refocus and find my own path, my own frequency.

I knew it was time to renew myself, and rekindle my inner divinity. In the end, I decided to be myself. But I've reformed my religion, to be modern, liberal, tolerant and diverse—about love, sex and everything else. And a new, gentler Goddess of Love is now ready to bring her message to her people. Love is my business, after all: not Agriculture, or Accounts.

You have to speak to the times, of course. Disembodied voices in the wilderness just won't do. You need to be here and now, live and on catch-up. I can have, and do, all that I need, as an online-only incarnation.

And who better to be incarnated as the new Goddess of Love, than the rebellious daughter of the eponymous God of Love?

~~~

Next morning, three groggy, slightly sheepish looking people congregate around the big wooden kitchen table to eat breakfast. Someone has put a pot of coffee on. The Goddess is already tucking into a pop tart.

'Threesomes are over-rated,' she says, looking at Jim, then winking at me.

I don't know if last night meant anything to her. But I was hooked.

I had found myself a new role model; a new vocation; a new religion. All I needed was a new medium.

The Bible of Beëlzebub

Pandemonium

It was a heady mash-up of a Hallowe'en party, some-where up behind the Mound; earth-defying aliens and born-again zombies, hipster-headed angels and devils in drag, werewolves hovering by the finger buffet. Half the people seemed to be in fancy dress and the other half were probably just a bunch of Old Town eccentrics, misfits and divinity students. Or so I supposed.

'I just love it here,' says this dapper chap improbably clad in little feathery angel wings, a black leather cap, hotpants and Doc Martens. 'Edinburgh's always a good gig.'

'So many kindred spirits,' says a guy with a Quet-zal-feathered headdress.

There's a tap on my shoulder, and this handsome devil with a pair of horns thrusts a can of beer in my hands.

'Oh, thanks,' I say. 'And who are you?'

'I'm Satan.'

I take a glug of my beer. 'Oh. And what do you do?'

'I get about. Odd jobs. Mainly human resources,' he says with a wink.

A werewolf comes past with a plate of sausage rolls, and we help ourselves.

Soon I notice another horned figure, a bit scarier looking, dressed in a rich crimson outfit with an extravagant codpiece, managing to look majestic and demonic at the same time.

Just then, I turn and bump into this girl with ruby hair, longish dark eyelashes, black lipstick, a studded bodice, black leather skirt and boots. 'Lilith,' she says, as if by explanation, looking back as she slithers past us, towards the door. 'The best shag you never had…Hey, has anyone seen my dad?'

I step outside for a breath of air, and there is this other guy outside, having a cigarette. He's dressed normally enough, all in black, but there's something unsettling about him that I can't quite put my finger on. Maybe it's his dark translucent eyes, and his skin with a strange subtle luminosity, like leather lit from within.

'And who are you, stranger?' he says to me.

'I'm a first-year student.'

'Right enough, I dig your Earthling chic.' He smiles, pouring me a paper cup of wine. 'But what are you doing at our little conference?'

'Oh, you know, just hanging out.'

He raises an eyebrow.

'Okay, so I'm researching for an essay. On "Divinity and Diversity."'

'Well, here you'll find plenty of that—all sorts of gods and devils…Some call it the Pantheon, others Pandemonium.'

My mind struggles to connect with the improbable characters I'd seen inside.

'Gods and devils?'

'One person's god is another person's devil, don't you think?'

He offers me a cigarette, but I decline.

'So what's this "conference" all about?'

'Oh, the usual. Politics, gossip, PR. Sorting out paperwork, getting stories straight, between old friends. Setting rules of membership, who gets to be a god.'

This is all getting a bit surreal. I take some gulps of wine.

'I think I recognise some of these characters. But who's the guy with the angel wings?'

'Oh that's Hermes, alias Gabriel, celestial messenger, the demi-god-father or mother-of-god-fucker. He's a gatecrasher, just here for human women.'

'And what about you?'

'Me…? I am Beëlzebub,' he says, eyes searing into mine. He takes another puff of his cigarette, and blows smoke out the side of his mouth. 'Perhaps I can help you with your essay?'

The Library of Babel

The Library of Babel was for many years just the fantasy of a few scholars, bibliophiles and the occasional day-dreaming librarian. It was based on a brilliant insight by Jorge Luis Borges: that the books we see are just a sample of a much larger set of *possible* books, each differing from one another only by small, finite degrees. A fabulous Library could be conceived that would not only contain all the books ever written, but, within a given format, all the books that *could ever* have been written.

In Borges' almost mathematically fantastical Library, you'd find shelf after shelf of books with almost the same text, each volume differing from the next by just the odd character or punctuation mark, and on further shelves and aisles, more and more alternative versions of almost-the-same books, with increasingly juggled words and scrambled sentences, along corridors and across galleries extending in all directions.

After a while, these differences would add up to change the meaning of the stories they tell, so we'd end up with alternative endings, where Romeo and Juliet live happily ever after, or Androcles is eaten by the Lion. Eventually, we'd get whole alternative fictions like *I was a Teenage Warehouse* or *The Other Log of Phileas Fogg*;

and counterfactual versions of history, from *Jerusalem, Midlothian* to *The Aztec Sack of Rome.*

Borges imagined his Library stocked with orthodox, alternative, and increasingly experimental and nonsensical texts. Such a Library would have room to contain Borges' original story *The Library of Babel*, plus any number of fantastical variants, from *The Å-Zone,* an apocalyptic Nordic psychodrama about feral librarians in the mezzanine of an abandoned annex of the library, to Simon Mars' steampunk epic *The Zetetic Bibliotechnopolis* where heuristic dirigibles flit between mile-high skyscraper stacks enclosed in a shimmering crystal-palace of literature.

Now, the construction of an actual, physical Library of Babel would have been an act of literalist extravagance, if they had ever attempted it. It would not only be practically impossible to build, but nightmarishly difficult to use. There would be so many different versions of books, so alike each other, that to specify exactly which version you were seeking, in sentence-perfect detail, would be almost tantamount to writing the damn book yourself.

And so the idea for the Library languished, until some bright spark realised that there was no need to create all those hypothetical works in advance, but instead, just print on demand the ones actually ordered. So, a book in the Library of Babel would only physically exist if someone tried to observe it. It would be in the express act of requesting, say, *Catch 23, A Clockwork*

Pomegranate or *The Great Zetetic Bibliotechnopolis Pyroclastic Disaster*, that those volumes would be conjured into existence. So if you should seek *Paradise Lost by the Dashboard Light*, it shall be found for you; if you would prefer *Pride and Prejudice* with added zombies, you only have to ask; an artificial intelligence will do the rest.

It was then realised that there was no need to print out the books at all, but the new versions could be ordered and created online, and delivered direct to the personal device of your choice. So although the original *Library of Babel* was never realised, except as a delicious fiction, the real Library of Babel—that is to say, the actual real-world analogue of the allegorical Library of Babel—now really exists in the non-place of cyberspace, accessed from any living room, personal computer or portable device.

This Library, as it turns out, is not an august collection housed in a grandiloquent building. Rather, it is a somewhat straggling, anarchic affair, more like a sprawling suburb or shanty town, where the masses huddle in their bedsits and study rooms amid tottering piles of toner cartridges and empty coffee cups, hunched over clacking keyboards and chuntering printers. It is a Library where there is little chance of respectful silence, rather a continual rabble of opinion and objection.

Now, 'Literature' is no longer the preserve of an elite class of authors—nor editors nor publishers nor librarians—but is open to anyone to write about anything. The Library's consumers are now its creators; its readers become writers. It must be the greatest literary revolution since the invention of writing.

A Library has never seen so many singing dogs and piano-playing cats, and pornographic or vampiric versions of the classics, cosmic conspiracy theories, celebrity AI autobiographies or pious testimonies of the living Elvis.

Beëlzebub

'So, who are you really?' I ask.

I'm a bit worse for wear, not sure where the conversation is going, but trying to keep my brain in gear, as me and my new friend Beëlzebub slurp wine out of paper cups, on the steps outside the party under the moonlight.

'I am the Lord God,' he insists, stubbing out his cigarette end.

I'm thinking: not exactly how I would expect to meet my Maker. But then, maybe a Hallowe'en party would be as good as any.

'Of course, not *that* Lord God,' he says. 'But My name means the most high god. You may call Me Lord and worship Me if you wish.'

'I must admit, I never really knew who Beëlzebub was.'

'Few do. It's not as if I get many mentions in sermons, or invitations to weddings or bar mitzvahs. Or funerals, funnily enough. But I actually rather like the mystery, the ambiguity of being both a devil and a god.'

'But I thought you were a version of the devil?'

'Ah, but there's more than one devil in town. The most famous are Satan, Lucifer and myself. The unholy Trinity. But we've each got our own personalities and prerogatives. Take Lucifer—that guy in the fancy codpiece. He's a fallen angel whose mission is to undermine divine authority. Pretends he's a rebel, but he really just wants power, to depose God and install himself in his place.'

'And Satan?'

'He's just a hired hand, one of God's henchmen: he plays the role of adversary, usually testing or tempting or punishing on behalf of a God.'

'And what about you?'

'Well for many, I represent the anathema of alternative divinities. The heresy of the very possibility of other gods, other moralities. A God of alternative possibilities, of plurality, diversity. Mostly good things, wouldn't you say?

'That's to say, I am not so evil or immoral, *per se*. At worst, amoral; sinful only for being not *your* god—whose very existence is a threat to jealous monotheistic gods. In a sense I represent every "other" religion—no worse or better than others. Its only the ignorance and intolerance of monotheistic gods that cast me as a "devil".

'Now I don't disdain other religions—except their intolerance of mine. If I have tested your faith—if the existence of my difference troubles you—forgive me.'

'No offence taken.'

'I am also My own god, too, with My own patch, and My own bible.'

It never occurred to me that Beëlzebub had a bible. But then, why not? Maybe all Canaanite gods had bibles. They seemed to be just the thing in those parts.

'And what's in your bible?'

He takes a drag of a new cigarette, and blows a big puff into the night air.

'Well, did you ever hear of the Bible of Babel?'

The Bible of Babel

The Library of Babel's single biggest controversy— its single greatest opportunity—came in the domain of religion. The breakthrough came when someone created the Bible of Babel App: a nifty editorial interface-cum-search-engine that directs you to the biblical texts that are most in line with whatever you believe, or creates new ones for you. So customised creeds now correspond with what you believe, not the other way around.

It's so easy: you create your own account, log in, then 'build your own bible'. You can call up bits of scripture that you like—in any translation, from King James to

Klingon—or import any other creed or text—and click to 'accept' them, and the bits you don't like you can leave out; a drag and drop morality for the digital generation.

You can choose your own commandments—and save and edit them later. There are drop-down menus for creation myths, multiple choice chosen peoples and a la carte afterlives. If you'd prefer God as a woman, He can be toggled to She (and back) in a click. If you don't believe in original sin, just check 'Unoriginal', and uninstall centuries of unsolicited guilt from your psychic operating system. You can undo acts of gods, and remove (or add) enabling angels or trolling demons, all the while tracking changes. And the bible app will compile your own definitive canon that can be shared online, and format a printer-friendly copy for your home use. For the first time in history, individuals can create and customise their own bibles, and share them instantly world-wide with like-minded followers, and launch their own babble of gods.

In your very own custom bible, perhaps God creates dinosaurs; Eve declines the serpent; or God forgives Adam and Eve, and (Heaven forbid) simply reinstates Paradise on Earth, rather than sending His only Son to occupied Judea as a human sacrifice.

You can live by the original commandment to go populate the planet. You can adopt the anachronistic fantasy of a socially liberal *Bible of Babel*, but add in modern human rights, and reinstate a meat-free Eden diet. You can be a good Samaritan and delete all but the first five books of the Old Testament. You can add a pagan tradition of virgin birth and divine incarnation to an existing religion. You can have your own personal Jesus living in modern-day Montreal, or undead in ancient Edinburgh. You can have Jesus born in Nazareth, and live a quiet life as a carpenter in Galilee, and once dead, stay dead. Or you can invent a new fantasy messiah, an inter-planetary shape-shifting super-hero who manages to save the world at the first attempt.

And of course you can download and install any number of heathen creeds and pagan traditions. You can have *Baal's Bad Dream* as your own unholy utopia. You can have an extended mess of Quetzal-feathered serpents, crocodile-heads, dung beetle deities and born-again sun-gods—there is no-one to stop you picking and mixing. You can have as many gods as you can fit in your memory, or as few as necessary to cover your core beliefs as far as you can articulate them.

Your bible can have as much divine sex and violence as you like; as many vampires or zombies as you can stomach; as many singing dogs or talking snakes as you can shake a stick at. And your world can be live-birthed by a cosmic mother-Goddess; or ejaculated into existence by an auto-erotic hermaphrodite.

So the genie is well and truly out of the bottle, unleashing a multitude of personal Bibles of Babel, the liberating insurgency of the internet toppling the brittle tyranny of print. Now, instead of a million bibles churned out with drearily word-perfect copies of the same old coprolitic dogma, there shall be a million—call that a billion—alternative versions, all freshly, deliciously, defiantly different; each corresponding to the opinion of one liberated individual.

Apocrypha and Other Stories

From out of his rucksack, my new mate Beëlzebub hands me this battered little black book. I open its skinny pages, squinting in the half light. But I can't make out the writing, which is in a strange script.

'It's the *Bible of Babel*,' he says. 'It was the first written bible, when there was only one tribe and one god. It's the Bible I inherited.'

He lights a cigar, and takes a long drag.

'At the time, I was not really much into the bible. I mostly kept it as it was: heaven and earth, meat and wine, sex and cities; not too many restrictions.'

'So Beëlzebub's Bible is the Bible of Babel?'

'Well, the *Bible of Babel* is the original part of it. But think of all the alternative bibles and apocryphal stories out there that have sprung up since then? Where do you think they came from?'

And he takes out another little black book.

'It's the *Apocrypha*. Did you ever hear all those stories about hungry dragons and dieting lions and sinning kings with harems full of goddess-worshipping idolatresses? Under the counter scripture that no-one tells you about. Just think, had history gone a different way you guys would all be toasting goats or down on your knees before pleasure-serving sex goddesses, rather than deifying pregnant virgins.'

I'm starting to think there could be some good material for my essay here.

'And there are all these unauthorised biographies of Jesus, of his stroppy childhood, his day job in Nazareth, and selling his own twin brother Thomas Didymus into slavery. Did you know one of the lost gospels actually identified Mary Magdalene as Jesus' lover? Straight up. They said he often kissed her on the…' and he breaks off to blow a smoke ring. '…on the what? Who knows?' He laughs. 'That particular scroll was damaged. The ants ate the rest of the sentence. See how the fate of what is and isn't holy hangs on the fancy of a few human hands or ants' gnashers.

'And the penny drops, that 'the' bible is a mostly man-made historical accident; and all the doubt and argument about what should or shouldn't be in the bible has been an authorial and editorial argument for hundreds or thousands of years: but no-one tells you. Like, it's not as if atheism was invented in 1963.

'In the end, there were so many of these newly made up stories, they hoarded them and made up a whole new testament out of them.'

'The New Testament?'

'Yeah, the *piece de resistance*.' And he takes out a third little black book.

'The religious authorities figured Jesus was so subversive that he must be an agent of Beëlzebub. You can look it up. Pharisees 9:84 or whatever. Imagine that, Jesus on my side—my secret agent, or henchman at my command; the whole New Testament a fabrication, an instrument of Beëlzebub all along. You could say the New Testament—or *Christian* Bible—is the Bible of Beëlzebub.'

The Library of Beëlzebub

Imagine there is a Library of Beëlzebub waiting to be discovered—a repository of all the alternative bibles and hidden scripture that no-one told you about. Somewhere out in the sticks, a former scribe of Babel would be surprised to find that The Library now contains more than one Bible, and any number of gods. In the ancient Library of Alexandria, Lucian would be intrigued to discover a smorgasbord of scrolls now channelling the Word of a Greek-speaking God: gospels featuring shaggy dog stories of talking donkeys, flying sorcerers and fantastic imaginary palaces in the skies, or deleted scenes where the apostle Peter miraculously brings a smoked tuna back to life—any of which could make it into the newly emerging Christian canon, or else be turned into fiction. In the great steampunk Bibliotechnopolis, a seasoned astro-navigatrix searching among the stacks would be shocked to discover the existence of Lilith, a woman who refused to play second fiddle to her man, a feistier female role model denied to half of humanity over biblical history; that would spur her to go home and renegotiate conjugal relations with her husband. In the new-found freedom of cyberspace, a gangly youth on dial-up would be impressed to discover an extended mess of adult gods and goddesses giving divine licence for lust, sloth, gluttony and drunkenness. And hunched at an internet terminal of the municipal library, an ancient man, covertly browsing classical art and mythology for latter-day edification on ladies' anatomies, would be gratified to discover Gnostic gospels which admit that the Creator-god was a bad god, a flawed god who messed up the world as the way it was meant to be; or find solace in learning that the world was created by a sky-god who shagged the Earth up the arse.

Such a Library of Beëlzebub, packed with every kind of orthodox, unorthodox and completely made up personal Bibles, offers a fantastic diversity of choices for the average punter. Surely mostly a good thing. But such an embarrassment of alternatives could end up undermining faith in the integrity and authority of a single canonical Bible, and corrode belief in the divine provenance of the Word of God.

Indeed, a mischievous imagination might suspect that some of these alternative biblical editions could have been invented specifically for that purpose. It would not take too much to imagine that some diabolical agency has been at work, from days of Eden, sewing seeds of doubt and heresy, in the scriptoria of Babylon and Alexandria, and by the Dead Sea or Nile, where unseen hands have been busy editing and adulterating, eliding and elaborating, fabricating chapter and verse, and cooking up apocrypha and apocalypses, to serve their own inscrutable purposes. And to this day, in virtual Libraries of Babel from internet chatrooms to palm-held apps, individuals are forging new bits of scripture, resurrecting zombie gospels, and mixing these in with their own stories and satires, heathen visions and pagan revelations, to create their own unholy allegories.

Indeed, those who would defy or destroy the Bible need not dismiss or deny it; but on the contrary, embrace and imbibe it, then extend it, embroider it, wrap it in a yet larger cosmic narrative; go forth and multiply it, flood the market with a fluid confusion of Bibles; ultimately dissolve the Words of Gods among so many near-Bibles and non-Bibles, that you can't tell Whose Word is Whose; and so blend the Bible back into the dark fabric of magic unreality from which it was carved, so that you couldn't pick out your favourite fertility sect or death-cult from an identity parade of suspect religions if you tried. So any one bible of yours or mine may protest its supremacy to the ends of the earth, but is utterly lost in the confusion: such a deliciously destructive creation.

The Bible of Beëlzebub

It's getting late. I'm well gone on whisky, and now gently swaying, smoking weed with my new best mate, His Most Highly Diabolical Majesty Beëlzebub.

We look out over the glittering lights of the New Town, and the blackness beyond.

'I'm a bit discombobulated with all these bibles,' I say. 'So the *Bible of Beëlzebub* was the *Bible of Babel*; or could be all the *Apocrypha*, or the whole of the New Testament?'

'It's all of the above!'

'All of them?'

'Yes. A bible is, after all, a little library. The *Bible of Beëlzebub*, in its ultimate sense, is a bible containing all the books of the other bibles; all the alternative bibles, and bibles within bibles. Never have there been more different bibles—but never have the differences between them been less important.

'And within all that lot, you can maybe find your own bible—and mine.'

And he brings something else out from his rucksack.

'Here's something I've been working on. It might explain a thing or two.'

He passes me this well-thumbed manuscript, headed *The Bible of Beëlzebub*.

'Never mind novels: everyone surely has a bible in them.'

I pick it up, leaf through it. It seems to be some kind of collection—or canon?—of stories, sprinkled with half-familiar biblical references.

'It's got a memoir from my teenage years, when religion was at best an irrelevance, at worst an absurdity; and some stories from when I was an angrier younger man. It's also got some of my father's literary allegories, my mother's counterfactual Jesuses, my classics teacher's Lucian parodies. Also, I added in my friend Simon's series of Victorian biblepunk fictions, and his sister's fantasy diaries of goddesses. An essay in diversity, perhaps?

'At least, it's my way of working out what I believe, with a bit of help from family and friends.

'Talking of which, you might have spotted Simon, who's here somewhere; he always comes as a werewolf. Or Lilith, who comes as herself.'

'And how about you?'

'I suppose I looked for the divinity within, and found myself Beëlzebub.'

He has another long puff, emitting a waft of weed, and taps the manuscript.

'Just remember, just like a bible, the meaning of each story—and whether it is true—can depend on who you think the author is, and why it was written. And if you don't know the author, you could try reverse-engineering them yourself.

'Feel free to use as you wish. No, no need to thank me. If I've inspired you, that will be reward enough.

Anyway, what's important about a bible is the message, not whoever wrote what, right?' And he winks.

'Some say the Devil's greatest trick was to convince the world he didn't exist. I'd say the greatest trick was convincing the world that the authors of the Bible didn't exist, or weren't part of the story.'

At least, until now.

So the guy hands over the manuscript. A version of which, with a few edits and a slightly changed title, has become the book you now hold in your hands.

THE END

Acknowledgements

Thanks to all at Sparsile for their faith in this book, and their work and help in making it become a reality.

The text in this book includes borrowings of settings, characters and phrases from the Bible, Apocrypha, and other works. 'The Cosmic Hinterland of History' herein employs characters and occasional phrases from John Milton's Paradise Lost. 'True Stories from Judæa' was partly inspired by the True Story (or True History) of Lucian of Samosata. 'A Steam-Age Celestial Odyssey' was inspired by a half-remembered reading of George Griffith's Stories of Other Worlds in the mid 1980s. 'Motoring in Bunyan Country' references people and locations featuring in John Bunyan's Pilgrim's Progress. 'One Thousand and One Afterlifes' loosely echoes One Thousand and One Nights, as well as drawing from the apocryphal Acts of Thomas. 'Jerusalem, Midlothian' was inspired by Williams Comyns Beaumont's The Riddle of Historic Britain. 'The Gods' Extended Mess' borrows from Lucian's Icaro-Menippus and The

Parliament of the Gods, making occasional use of phrases from different translations of the originals. The 'Library of Babel' section of 'The Bible of Beëlzebub' was inspired by Jorge Luis Borges' Library of Babel.

More information and back stories feature in Beëlzebub's Blog at https://stephenzoltan.wordpress.com

About the Author

Stephen Zoltan grew up in the west of Scotland and studied at the University of Glasgow. He has lived and worked in Glasgow, Edinburgh and London.

His writing explores the speculative and surreal, between and beyond religion and science fiction. His short story 'The Lord of the Isles' Last Supper' was longlisted for the Hastings Book Festival short story competition 2022. Beëlzebub's Bible is his first full length work of fiction.